'Look, Julian, I *know* why you walked out on me, and I admit it hurt at the time. But I'm over that now. I had a lot of adjustments to make after I found out I'd never dance again, never even walk straight again, for God's sake.' Claudia took a deep breath. 'But I don't blame you any more. You're an artist, a seeker after perfection. I understand that when you found out I would be a cripple the rest of my life, you simply didn't want anything more to do with me.'

'It's not at all what you think. I know it looked like that, but believe me, it wasn't. God, you're stubborn,' he said in an exasperated tone. 'What do I have to do to make you listen to me? Damn it, I *like* you, I'm very attracted to you. Won't you at least give me a chance to explain?'

ONE STOLEN MOMENT

BY

ROSEMARY HAMMOND

MILLS & BOON LIMITED
ETON HOUSE 18-24 PARADISE ROAD
RICHMOND SURREY TW9 1SR

All the characters in this book have no existence outside the imagination of the Author, and have no relation whatsoever to anyone bearing the same name or names. They are not even distantly inspired by any individual known or unknown to the Author, and all the incidents are pure invention.

All Rights Reserved. The text of this publication or any part thereof may not be reproduced or transmitted in any form or by any means, electronic or mechanical, including photocopying, recording, storage in an information retrieval system, or otherwise, without the written permission of the publisher.

This book is sold subject to the condition that it shall not, by way of trade or otherwise, be lent, resold, hired out or otherwise circulated without the prior consent of the publisher in any form of binding or cover other than that in which it is published and without a similar condition including this condition being imposed on the subsequent purchaser.

*First published in Great Britain 1988
by Mills & Boon Limited*

© Rosemary Hammond 1988

*Australian copyright 1988
Philippine copyright 1988
This edition 1988*

ISBN 0 263 75993 8

*Set in Palacio 10 on 11 pt.
01-0688-58961*

Typeset in Great Britain by JCL Graphics, Bristol

*Printed and bound in Great Britain by
Collins, Glasgow*

CHAPTER ONE

CLAUDIA awoke that morning to a pleasant chirping sound. She listened for a moment, then opened her eyes, blinking at the shaft of sunlight pouring in through the window. It was the first fine day in early April, and the robins were building their new nests high up in the tall fir tree outside her bedroom window.

Slowly and carefully, she eased herself out of bed, limped over to the window and opened it wide. The thunderous sound of the incoming tide pounding against the rocks below and the fresh smell of the tangy salt air filled the crisp morning air. She stretched widely, then hugged herself. The sun would do wonders for her little garden, she mused lazily, and for the first time since she'd arrived at her brother's house after the accident last autumn the familar, sickening load on her heart seemed just a shade lighter.

Then, as she turned back to get dressed, her eye was caught by the letter still lying on her dresser where she'd put it yesterday, and the gloom threatened once again.

Last night she had promised her brother she'd reconsider her decision to decline the offer of a teaching post with her old dance company, that she would sleep on it before taking definite action. But now, sickened by the mere sight of the envelope, she knew she'd made the right choice. She'd tell him this morning.

By the time breakfast was over, the dicussion had gradually escalated from calm disagreement to heated words, and finally into a fullblown shouting match, with Claudia and Peter glaring across the table at each other, both of them virtually quivering with fury, so angry by now that they could barely speak, while poor Laura sat at her place between them with eyes firmly fixed on her plate, looking smaller by the moment.

Finally, Peter threw down his napkin and rose abruptly to his feet to the tune of a loud clatter of crockery as he knocked over his coffee mug. There was utter silence in the sunny breakfast-room, except for the steady drip, drip of the spilled coffee as it flowed from the tabletop on to the red tile floor.

'I never said I wanted you to leave,' Peter ground out at last. 'I only said I thought you should consider the offer. Believe it or not, sister dear, I was only thinking of your welfare.'

'I don't want to teach,' Claudia said in a flat, dull tone. 'Why can't you understand? If I can't dance, I don't ever want to go near the theatre or the company again.'

Peter opened his mouth, shut it again and gave her an exasperated look. Then he turned on his heel and stomped heavily out of the room. When he was gone, Claudia's fingers loosened their grip on the edge of the table, and she slumped forwards, elbows on the table, her head in her hands.

As she calmed down, she began to feel a little guilty about Laura, still sitting spechless and immobile at her side. She turned to her sister-in-law, intending to apologise first and then offer to clean up the still quietly dripping coffee, but, when she saw Laura's mouth twitching with suppressed laughter, she had to smile herself.

'I'm sorry, Laura,' she said with a sigh. 'Peter and I have argued like that all our lives, but it's too bad we had to bring you in on it. Bad manners, too.' She pushed back her chair. 'I'll get the mop from the kitchen.'

Laura held out a restraining hand. 'Not to worry,' she said cheerfully. 'Mrs Jacobs comes to clean today. It'll give her something to do besides push dust around and pass on the local gossip.' The hand came to rest on Claudia's arm. 'You surely understand that Peter and I both want you to stay as long as you like. I mean that sincerely, and I know he does, too.'

Claudia nodded. 'I do know that, Laura, and I'm grateful. But I'm not exactly destitute, you know. The woman whose car hit me was well insured and, since the accident was clearly her fault, the company has paid up without a murmur.'

'Well, I'm glad you're well taken care of, but this is your home, too, after all. Even though the ranch was left outright to Peter, it was with the provision that you would always have a home here.'

'Oh, I know I have the legal right . . .'

Laura withdrew her hand. 'Now, listen here, Claudia. Do you want to get into a quarrel with me, too? Legal be damned! We both *want* you here.'

Claudia could only stare. Her normally calm, placid sister-in-law's face was flushed brick-red, and her pale blue eyes flashed with fire.

'I'm sorry, I'm sorry!' she cried, raising both hands in the air. Then, with a smile, she added, 'I seem to be stepping on everyone's toes this morning. Maybe I'd better leave before Mrs Jacobs arrives and I get into it with her as well.'

Gradually, Laura's complexion returned to its normal colour. She pushed back a stray stand of grey hair and gave Claudia a sheepish grin. 'Let's just forget it,' she said, rising to her feet. 'Do you have a therapy session today?'

'No, thank goodness. It's such a beautiful morning, I thought I'd go down to the pond and get some work done on the garden.'

'Well, that's a form of therapy, I guess. The walk itself is good exercise, but you mustn't overdo it with the heavy work. Peter can loan you one of the men for that.'

Claudia got up and began to collect the breakfast dishes. 'I can manage,' she said. 'Besides, I want it to be all my own project.'

Laura worked in silence beside her, gathering up the silverware and folding the napkins. After a few moments she turned to Claudia and gave her a look of concern.

'How is it?' she asked quietly. 'Any improvement at all?'

Claudia glanced sharply at her, then forced out a laugh. 'Well, obviously, I'll never dance again, but other than that, I do manage to get around with less trouble all the time.'

Not for worlds would she utter a word to either her brother or his wife about the crippling cramps that seized her bad leg in the middle of the night, or the many times she'd fallen on her way to the pond because the wasted muscles would not do her bidding, or the excruciating therapy sessions that left her limp and exhausted. The physical pain was nothing to her, anyway, compared to the stark fact that her life as a dancer was over.

'How's the garden coming?' Laura asked as they carried the breakfast things into the kitchen.

'Well, it won't win any prizes in a landscaping competition, but I'm finding my thumb isn't quite as brown as I'd imagined. In fact, the hyacinth bulbs I planted last autumn are actually going to bloom. I'm hoping the sun might bring a few of them out today.'

'It's a lovely setting for a garden, too,' Laura remarked as she rinsed off plates. 'Right next to the pond, with all the trees and the channel and the other islands in the background.'

Claudia, who had never had a moment's interest in gardening in her life before her accident, had to smile at the note of earnest encouragement in Laura's tone. It had taken the combined efforts of the doctor, the therapist, and both her brother and his wife to convince her that she needed some mild physical occupation to help build back the muscular mobility of her shattered leg.

She felt a sudden wave of love for the small, plump, grey-haired woman, who was busying herself at the sink now, her eyes averted. Both Laura and Peter were quite a few years older than Claudia, in their forties. She had intruded into their quiet lives once more like a sullen bombshell and, except for the occasional row with Peter, they both had treated her with unremitting affectionate care from the moment she arrived.

'Laura,' she said with a sigh, 'you're so good and I'm such an ungrateful beast. Let me at least wash up these dishes.'

'No, thanks. Mrs Jacobs can do them. I'm going to drive into the village this morning to do some shopping. Is there anything I can pick up for you?'

'Well, if you have time, you might take a look at

some primrose plants at the nursery. I noticed in the evening paper that they just got in a new shipment. They'll go well with the hyacinths.'

The Hamilton family sheep ranch was set high on the crest of a hill in the middle of Orcas Island, one of the San Juan group midway between the Washington coast and Canada's Vancouver Island, and sheltered both from the periodic storms that raged out of the Pacific Ocean to the west and the winds that swept down from the Cascade Mountains to the east.

As Claudia picked her way cautiously down the rocky slope to the pond, stopping every few yards to rest her leg, she was struck once again by the beauty of her surroundings, the small green islands rising like emeralds out of the deep blue water of the wide channels that wound around them, the fresh, clean air, the utter stillness.

By the time she reached the small plot of ground Peter had set aside for her to work, she was out of breath and perspiring. One of the ranch hands had built a wire fence around the area to keep out the grazing sheep, and she went through the small wooden gate, closing it firmly behind her. It was lambing time, and the woolly infants had a habit of wandering off in to uncharted territory, the ewes bleating closely behind them. Once they got beyond the fence, the carefully tended garden would become a mere mid-morning snack for the voracious creatures.

The garden was located at the extreme north-west corner of her brother's property, near a U-shaped pond that was shared with a neighbour. In the centre of the U was a large stand of fir and cedar that blocked off the outer edges of the pond and gave

Claudia the privacy she craved.

It wasn't until she had knelt down to inspect the budding hyacinth for traces of colour that she noticed that the man in the field next door was back. He had been gone for several weeks, then it had rained steadily throughout most of March, and she'd almost forgotten about him.

He'd been working on his side of the low stone fence that separated the two properties ever since she'd come back to Hidden Harbour last autumn. For the most part, he had been screened from view behind the clump of evergreens at the bend of the pond, and so far away that, in the beginning, he had only been a small figure in the distant landscape.

As the autumn and winter had progressed, however, he had moved steadily closer to the fence. Although Claudia had scrupulously ignored him, she did notice that his only occupation seemed to be felling some of the older trees on his property, chopping up the logs and loading them on to the back of a dilapidated pick-up truck every afternoon when he was finished.

They had never spoken. At first he had been too far away, but now, as each day brought him a little nearer the boundary, Claudia began to resent his intrusion on her solitude, and she made it a point to keep her eyes firmly averted and her head down to avoid having to acknowledge his presence.

As she glanced at the man now out of the corner of her eye, she felt a spurt of annoyance. He was dressed as he had been all winter, in worn jeans and a heavy woollen shirt. He wore gloves, boots, a cap on his head, and his face was covered with a thick black beard.

Then suddenly, before she could look away, their

eyes met, and in spite of the beard and the fact that they were still more than a hundred yards apart, there was no mistaking the harsh, shut-in look he gave her, a look that clearly mirrored her own thoughts. In that split second it was obvious that he was as annoyed by her presence as she was by his.

Quickly she lowered her eyes, grabbing her trowel and began to stab viciously at the earth around the tender plants. In the process, she knocked off the thickest, plumpest hyacinth bud. She could have wept with frustration. Somehow it seemed to be all his fault, and she fought down the urge to throw her trowel at him.

The lovely morning was ruined. First the argument with Peter, now this. Tears of self-pity welled up behind her eyes as she gazed down at the fast-wilting stalk lying in the dust.

That night, after dinner, Claudia decided to ask her brother about his bearded, taciturn neighbour. The evening had turned chilly as the sky clouded late that afternoon, and Peter had built a fire in the livingroom. Laura sat under the lamplight, working on one of her endless needlework projects for the local church bazaar, and Peter was scowling down at the account books spread before him on the coffee-table.

The room was quiet except for the click of Laura's needles, the crackling of the burning logs and an occasional groan from Peter as he turned the pages of his ledger.

'I've been meaning to ask you, Peter,' she said casually. 'Who has the property next door now?'

Peter looked up at her. 'You mean the old Carmichael place?' He glanced over at his wife. 'Some kind of artist, I think. What's his name,

Laura?'

Laura's needles stilled for a moment, and she gazed thoughtfully into the fire. 'Graves, isn't it?'

Claudia laughed. 'Don't you even know your own neighbours any more? I can't believe it. I thought surely everyone within miles would have his life history by now.'

Laura smiled at her. 'Well, he only came a year ago. Give us time.'

'All I know,' Peter put in, 'is that when he bought the place from the Carmichaels, the first thing he did was sell all the livestock and start cutting down trees.' He made a noise of disgust deep in his throat and shook his head. 'It's a damn shame. I hate to see all those old firs and cedars go. Some of them are over a hundred years old.'

'Maybe he plans to farm it,' Claudia suggested.

'Hah!' Peter snorted. 'I doubt it but, if so, I wish him luck. All this hilly terrain is good for is grazing. More for mountain goats even than sheep. Besides, it's so sandy and rock-infested, you'd never get anything to grow unless you filled in with several tons of topsoil.'

'Why do you ask, Claudia?' Laura said. 'Has he bothered you?'

'Oh, no. He keeps entirely to himself. He just suddenly appeared today while I was working in the garden and startled me, that's all.'

'You mean he spoke to you?' Laura sounded surprised. 'According to the village grapevine, he's not at all friendly.'

'No, he didn't speak to me. It's just that he hadn't been around for some weeks, and I didn't expect to see anyone. He's a rather forbidding-looking man, too, with that wild beard and those rough work-clothes.' She turned to her brother. 'You said he was an artist, Peter. What kind?'

Peter shrugged. 'Beats me. Probably one of those hippy types who splash on coloured polka dots or draw soup cans and call it art.'

'Is he still cutting down the trees?' Laura asked.

'Oh, yes,' Claudia replied. 'He's been out in his field off and on since last fall, and all I ever see him do is chop them down, saw them into logs and cart them off in his truck. He's really quite single-minded about the whole process, and,' she added with a laugh, 'very efficient.'

Peter scowled. 'You say he startled you? By God, if he touches one limb of a single tree on my property, I'll haul him into court so fast it'll make his head spin!'

'Oh, he's nowhere near the boundary yet,' Claudia assured him. 'And I've seen no sign that he covets your trees.' She smiled at him. 'Tell you what—if I see him cross the line, I'll send up a flare and you can come running with your shotgun.'

Muttering ominously under his breath, Peter returned to his books and the subject was dropped.

It was raining next morning, a steady, chilly downpour that continued throughout the whole day. As Claudia gazed out her window at the grey sky and sodden tree branches, she thought it was just as well. After yesterday's encounter with the silent Mr Graves, she didn't feel much like working in the garden, anyway. That sudden intrusion into her solitude had somehow dampened her pleasure in the work.

Besides, it was one of her bi-weekly therapy mornings, and that ordeal always left her worn out for the rest of the day. Jenny was due any minute now, and Claudia made it a point to greet her at the door. It was the least she could do. Since she was not able to drive yet, Jenny had to come to her.

By the time she had made her arduous way down the stairs to the hall, she could hear Jenny's car swishing on the pavement outside. She opened the door and stood on the covered porch, waiting for her while she parked the old blue Toyota and collected her bag.

'Sorry to get you out on such a filthy morning,' she called.

Jenny came running across the driveway and up the steps, her bright red curls glistening with raindrops. When she was under cover of the porch roof, she shook her head vigorously and brushed off the sleeves of her raincoat.

'No problem,' she said and gave Claudia one of her quick, bright grins. 'How's it going?'

'Not bad,' Claudia replied, and they went inside.

Jenny took off her coat and hung it on the hall tree, then turned and darted her a stern look. 'That's what you always say,' she commented accusingly. 'I'm not only one of your oldest friends, I'm also your therapist. You don't have to put on a front with me. Come on, now, the truth.'

'Well, this time I mean it. See?'

They started towards the sun lounge where the sessions took place. Jenny always walked a step or two behind Claudia so that she could observe the way she handled the bad leg.

'OK,' she said as when they got there. 'You're right. There is an improvement. Now, let's see you hop up by yourself.'

Claudia took off her robe and approached the

special raised table Peter had built and installed to Jenny's specifications, a wide wooden plank nailed to saw-horses and covered with a thin mattress with white sheeting. She sat down on the edge and awkwardly manoeuvred her legs up, biting her lip and scowling in concentration at the painful effort it took to perform even that simple task.

When it was over, Jenny clapped her hands in applause. 'Good for you! You've been practising, I see.' Gently, she eased Claudia's shoulders down on the mattress in a prone position, then leaned over and gazed down at her with a sober expression. 'Just the fact that you're finally trying is a huge step forward, Claudia,' she said softly.

'I know. I've been an awful patient, right from the beginning, haven't I?'

'No worse than any other. Don't you think I know what it cost you, of all people, to lose the use of a leg? But if I'd given you the sympathy I felt, you'd still be lying flat on your back, afraid to move. You've come a long way since last fall, Claudia, and I'm proud of you.' She straightened up briskly. 'Now, let's get to work.'

An hour later it was finally over, and while Claudia lay on the table, recuperating from the painful exercise, Jenny busied herself collecting her things. Then she came back to help her up to a sitting position and began to gently massage the sore leg.

'How's the garden coming?' she asked.

'Quite well.'

'Still working on it?'

Claudia nodded. 'Every day I can.'

'I think that's probably the real secret of your fine progress. Walking is still the best exercise of all. Just so long as you don't overdo it. What are you growing?'

Claudia slid down off the table, gingerly putting one foot after the other down on the floor. 'Well, the hyacinth bulbs I planted last fall look like they might actually bloom.' Then she laughed. 'But yesterday I managed to break off the most promising bud.'

'How in the world did you do that?'

'Oh, the next-door neighbour appeared out of the blue, and I zigged when I should have zagged.'

'You mean Julian Graves?'

Claudia's eyes widened. 'You know him? I thought he was the great mystery man of Hidden Harbour.'

'Not really, but I knew his wife. She was injured in much the same way you were, and for a while I gave her some mild massage therapy.' She shook her head sadly. 'But it was hopeless. She had other, more serious injuries and died less than a month after the accident.'

'How terrible!'

'Yes, it was. Not all my patients give me the lift you do.'

They walked together to the hall, where Jenny put on her raincoat and opened the door. It was still raining.

'What's he like,' Claudia asked, 'this Julian Graves?'

'Well, as I say, I didn't really know him, and I only worked with his wife for a few weeks. I hear he went to pieces after her death, just shut himself in the old Carmichael house and became a kind of recluse.'

'Peter said he's an artist of some kind.'

'Yes, quite a successful painter, from what I can gather.' She stepped out on to the porch. 'Well, I'll be off. I have a noon appointment on the other side of the island. Keep up the good work, and I'll see you on Friday. It won't be long before you'll be able to drive into the village yourself.'

She sprinted towards the Toyota, and with a last quick wave got inside and started the engine. Claudia stood on the porch, watching until the little blue car disappeared around the first bend in the winding road.

She went back inside and shut the door, just as Laura was emerging from the kitchen where she had been baking her weekly batch of bread. The loaves were in the oven now, and the whole house was beginning to fill with the warm, yeasty aroma.

'Is Jenny gone?' Laura asked, wiping her hands on her apron. 'I was going to ask her to stay for lunch.'

'She had another appointment,' Claudia said, moving towards her. She sniffed the air. 'The bread smells heavenly.'

'What did Jenny have to say?' Laura asked cautiously.

'About me?' Laura nodded. 'She said she sees great improvement. In fact, her parting words were that I'd soon be driving to town myself for our sessions.'

Laura's plump face was immediately wreathed in a broad smile. 'Oh, Claudia, I'm so pleased!'

'So am I. In fact, I was just on my way upstairs to finish my morning exercises.' She made a face. 'Nasty things.'

Laura laughed. 'Peter will be back for lunch in half an hour.'

'I'll be through by then.'

Upstairs, Claudia paused at the door to her bedroom, struck by a sudden thought. The first thing she had insisted on when she came back home was that the full-length mirror she used to practise in front of be removed from her bedroom, and it had been relegated to a small, unused bedroom just down the hall. On a sudden impulse, she continued down the corridor towards it.

Glancing guiltily over her shoulder, she opened the door. It was stuffy inside, the blinds drawn, dust collecting in the corners. Numerous cardboard boxes full of old clothes and her nephews' cast-off toys were stacked along the walls.

She switched on the overhead light and walked slowly over to the mirror, still leaning up against the wall where Peter had placed it months ago. Slipping off her robe, she stood and gazed at her reflection: the black leotard she wore for the therapy sessions, her long dancer's legs bare. In the dim light, the scars on her injured leg were not visible.

A choking sensation clutched at her throat. With her smooth black hair pulled back tightly into a knot at the top of her head, her slim, small-boned figure and high, firm breasts, she still looked like a dancer!

For a moment she could forget the accident, the weeks in the hospital, the long months of inactivity, the gruelling therapy. She flexed the muscles of her good right leg and raised her hands high above her head in the familiar graceful position. Slowly lifting herself on tiptoe, she tentatively put a little weight on the bad leg, testing its strength.

Immediately a sharp jab of pain shot through it. She reached out a hand against the mirror to break her fall, then slid to the floor and lay there, crumpled, her hands over her face, the tears streaming from her eyes.

If she needed any proof that her dancing days were over, this was it. The progress she had made went only so far. She would never dance again.

* * *

It rained steadily for an entire week. Depressed by her shattering experience at the mirror, Claudia could barely force herself to do her daily exercises, and spent most of her time moping around the house, reading or staring out the window at the dripping trees and leaden grey sky.

When the sun finally did reappear, on the following Wednesday, she was so sick of the four walls of the house and her own depressing thoughts that, immediately after breakfast, she set out for the garden, in spite of the fact that the ground was still oozing mud.

Peter was out in front tinkering with his car when she came outside, and as she passed by him he looked up and stared at her.

'You can't work in the garden in this mud,' he said flatly.

'Well, I can go look at it,' she replied with a defiant lift of her chin. She held up the small box of blooming primrose plants Laura had picked up for her at the nursery over a week ago.

'Besides, these poor posies are not happy in the house. I can at least get them in the ground.'

Peter only shrugged and stuck his head back under the hood of the car. Claudia sailed past him, disguising her limp as best she could, and continued on her way down the path that led to the meadow.

Although the grass was still wet underfoot and the trees still dripping, it was a fine day. She had put on her boots, but other than that one concession to the past week of rain, she wore only a pair of jeans and a thin, striped shirt, and the sun was warm on her face and arms.

After a week shut inside the house, the fresh air was bracing and exhilarating, slightly steamy and humid, but with a gentle breeze blowing up from the wide blue channel that separated Hidden Harbour from the neighbouring islands.

The wet grass was quite slippery, and she picked her way very carefully down the rocky slope, concentrating all her attention on balancing the tray of primroses and watching her footwork to avoid the potholes and larger stones.

Just as she came within sight of the small garden plot, some twenty feet away, she stopped to rest. As she raised her head, her eye was caught by a bright splash of colour sparkling among the greenery. One of the hyacinths had bloomed at last!

Without thinking, she hurried towards the garden. In the next step she took, her toe came up against a hidden rock, and she lurched forward. Unable to break her fall, she uttered a cry, the tray in her hands went flying, and the next thing she knew she was lying, sprawled face down, on the wet grass.

Since she had dimly sensed it coming, she had been able to cushion the fall somewhat with her good leg, and was more angry with herself than hurt. Still, the wind was knocked out of her, and she lay still for a moment, her eyes shut tight, while she caught her breath.

Suddenly, she felt herself being lifted up by a pair of strong arms. Her first thought was that Peter had followed her, but when she opened her eyes she found herself gazing up into the harsh countenance of Julian Graves.

She was so shocked at the apparition, the closeness of the heavy beard, the cold grey eyes, that she couldn't move, couldn't utter a sound. He wasn't wearing his cap today, and the thick, black hair, which looked as though it hadn't been cut for months, only made him seem fiercer, wilder, and much more menacing.

As she stared up at him, wide-eyed and speechless, the glower on his face began to soften imperceptibly, and she felt his arms tighten around her. Raising one heavy black eyebrow, his thin lips curled in a half-smile.

'Well, well,' he said. 'Look what I've caught. A wood nymph! Are you hurt?'

His voice was quite deep, yet softer than she had expected, and as she stared up into his eyes, a clear grey mottled with black flecks, she felt a strange sensation of warmth mingled with an underlying warning flash of apprehension.

'No,' she said, finding her voice at last. 'I'm fine. Please put me down.'

He didn't move a muscle. 'Are you always so clumsy?' he asked with the same wry smile. His glance flicked over her. 'You have a well made, athletic body. I would have expected a more graceful descent.'

With a swift rush of relief, she realised then that he had not noticed her limp. At the same time, it also dawned on her that her thin blouse was soaked through from the wet grass, and it was obvious just exactly how he had arrived at his conclusion about her body.

He was also holding her very tightly against his broad chest, so close that she could feel the beat of his heart against her bare arm, see the fine lines around his eyes and smell his clean outdoors scent.

He flashed her a wicked grin that revealed even white teeth, and bent his head towards her. 'I've always been partial to women with fragile bones and black hair,' he murmured.

Although she recognised the flash of desire, the coldness in the steely eyes frightened her. 'Please put me down,' she said shakily. 'I'm fine, really I am.'

His head continued coming down towards her and, just as his mouth was about to meet hers, she turned her head away so that his lips merely brushed against her cheek. When she felt the bristles of his beard, rough and rasping against her skin, she stiffened in his arms and began to struggle.

He raised his head abruptly and gave her a narrow-eyed, appraising look. Then his hold on her loosened, and he lowered her to her feet. Claudia turned away from him and began to brush the mud off her front. Relieved to be free of that strong grip, yet curious as to what he had in mind, she darted a quick sideways glance at him.

He was standing with his arms folded across his broad chest, towering over her, a distant expression on his lean, bearded face.

'Thank you for your concern,' she said hastily.

With one brief nod, he turned and stalked off across the meadow towards his own property. Claudia stood and watched the tall, straight figure, shoulders broad under the rough woollen shirt, hips slim in the worn blue jeans. At the stone fence, he braced one hand on the top and vaulted gracefully over to the other side.

He never once looked back, and in just a few moments he had disappeared from view.

CHAPTER TWO

THE fine weather continued and, although Claudia had half-heartedly considered giving up the garden entirely after that one embarrassing encounter with Julian Graves, the very next day she was back at work. Not only did she need the exercise, but she felt she had a responsibility now for the growing things she herself had planted.

Besides, she thought as she picked her way carefully down the slope, nothing had really happened. He'd made a pass at her, she'd resisted, he'd backed off and that was the end of it.

As it turned out, he wasn't there anyway, nor did he show up for the next few days. When he finally did return, they avoided each other by some unspoken agreement, without even a nod acknowledging the other's presence, and from then on they continued to pursue their own silent, lonely labours in their separate fields, as through they were a thousand miles apart or on different planets.

He was moving further away from the stone fence now. From time to time, Claudia managed to sneak a surreptitious look at him and, as she watched the tall form wielding the axe, her curiosity about him grew with each passing day.

He would raise the axe high above his head, then slam it down so viciously on the log at his feet that she could almost palpably feel the barely suppressed violence in the man, a silent rage that he expended

on the inert tree trunks and branches, and it
gradually occurred to her that his monotonous
chopping was as much a form of therapy for him as
the garden was for her.

She wondered what demon he was trying to
exorcise with his single-minded labours. Jenny had
mentioned a dead wife. Could he still be grieving for
her? On the other hand, perhaps the cold fury she
sensed in him was simply his normal personality.
Artists could be temperamental, subject to strange
mood swings that sometimes verged on manic
depression. She'd been around enough eccentric
dancers and musicians to know that.

He was an impressive-looking man, if a little
frightening with the unruly hair and wild beard. Now
that the weather was warmer, he would shed his
shirt by mid-afternoon when the sun was at its
hottest, and his strong back and shoulders grew
browner each day, glistening with perspiration as he
worked, the muscles rippling under the tanned skin.

More than once, she had to fight down a sudden
unexpected surge of longing, a pang of regret that he
had given up so easily on her. Whenever this
happened, she would have to convince herself firmly
once again that she'd been right to reject his
advances. Once he became aware of her ruined leg,
the unsightly scars, the awkward limp, he would
turn from her in disgust anyway.

The great day finally arrived when Claudia was ready
to attempt the drive into town by herself, and she
faced it with mingled delight and trepidation. When
Jenny made the announcement at their next session,
she immediately objected.

But Jenny had insisted. 'You're ready, Claudia.

Would I lie to you? You've got to trust me. Laura or Peter can go with you the first few times, if you like, at least until you feel more confident.'

'I don't know, Jenny,' Claudia demurred. 'I don't *feel* ready.'

'Believe me, you never will until you try it. Physically, your leg is strong enough. Besides, Peter's car has an automatic transmission. You won't even have to use your bad leg. And you won't have to drive to me *every* time—not yet, anyway.'

On the day of the maiden voyage, Laura agreed readily to go with her, since Peter suddenly found he had important matters to attend to at the ranch that morning. He did come outside to see them off, however, and as Claudia settled herself behind the wheel she gave him a dirty look.

'Important matters, my eye,' she said to him through the open window. 'You're just chicken.' She turned to Laura, seated calmly at her side. 'I noticed he doesn't mind sacrificing you.'

Laura only shook her head. Claudia started the engine, released the handbrake and started off down the driveway, leaving a worried-looking Peter standing behind, looking after them. As she turned on to the main road into town, she gave Laura a brief glance.

'I can't believe it! It's as though I never quit driving in the first place.'

'I think it's something like swimming,' Laura replied with a smile. 'Or riding a bicycle. Once you've learned, you never forget.'

The small village of Hidden Harbour was only a few miles from the ranch and consisted of one street, three blocks long, which ended sharply at the small marina and fishing dock. The boating season was just beginning to stir and, although it wouldn't come into full swing until after Memorial Day at the end of May, several shops had already opened up for the early fishermen.

With a sense of heady exhilaration, Claudia drove slowly past the familiar wooden buildings that lined the main street. 'Do you realise,' she said, 'that this is the first time I've even been to town since I came here last autumn? It all looks exactly the same as it did years ago.'

'Oh, things don't change much around here,' Laura said. She pointed to a wide space at the kerb. 'Why don't you pull up there in front of the grocery store?' Laura said. 'I have to order some things from Mr Jennings for the party.'

Claudia darted her a sharp look. 'What party?'

'You know, the party we always give at the end of April. We like to have it well before Memorial Day, before the vacationers arrive and while we still have the island to ourselves. Don't you remember?'

Claudia's eyes widened in horror. 'But that's only a couple of weeks off!'

'I know, dear.'

'But I can't . . .'

'Watch out!' Laura cried, and in the next instant there was a loud, sickening crunch of metal on metal, and a jolting thud rocked the car. Mindlessly, Claudia closed her eyes and slammed on the brakes at the same time, then sat there, trembling from head to foot, a cold perspiration breaking out over her whole body as memories of her own accident flooded painfully back into her mind.

Rigid with shock, every muscle tense, her clammy hands gripping the steering wheel, she sat there gasping for breath, until finally she became aware of

Laura's steadying hand on her arm and realised she was speaking to her in a low, soothing voice.

'It's all right, Claudia. Don't worry about it. No one's hurt. It's only a dented fender.'

Slowly, she opened her eyes to see Laura gazing at her with concern and still patting her arm. She expelled a great sigh and slumped back on the seat. It had all happened so fast! Just a second ago, it seemed, they'd been driving slowly along the street, chatting about the party . . . Oh, God, she groaned inwardly, the party! She didn't even want to think about the party!

Calmer now, she looked up through the front windscreen to see just what she'd done. Apparently, she'd drifted into the oncoming lane because there, straight ahead and slightly angled in front of them, sat a familiar blue pick-up truck.

'Oh, no,' she whispered as she saw the driver get out and slam the door behind him; then, in the next moment, a very angry Julian Graves came striding towards them.

'What the hell do you think you're doing, lady?' he barked as he approached. He leaned down to glare inside. 'Didn't you even look . . .'

He broke off. As their eyes met, the light of recognition dawned in the cold grey eyes, and he backed off a step. The stern look faded to a thin, humourless smile. He straightened up, long legs apart, knuckles resting on his hips, and stared down at her.

'Ah,' he said drily. 'The wood nymph. You drive about as gracefully as you walk, I see.'

Claudia's face went immediately up in flames. She couldn't speak. The shock of the collision, the draining after-effects, and now this bearded giant shouting at her, were all too much. She stared up at him, blinking helplessly. He had crossed his arms over his chest, and merely continued to stand there frowning down at her, obviously waiting for her to say something sensible.

Then her own temper began to rise. She couldn't just let him bully her like this, and he did seem to be over-reacting slightly. No one was hurt, after all, and clearly there was only minor damage done.

She raised her chin. 'You don't need to shout at me,' she said with dignity.

He took off his cap, ran a hand through the thick black hair and shook his head. 'You've got some nerve,' he said at last with grudging admiration. He put a hand on the door and started to pull it open. 'Just get out and take a look at what you did to my front headlight.'

Claudia froze. She couldn't get out of the car. It would kill her to have this man see her weakness, the ugly, awkward limp that distorted her whole body in a grotesque parody of her former grace.

Just then, Laura leaned across her and smiled up at the tall man. 'Oh, Mr Graves, I'm so sorry. It's really my fault. I'm afraid we got into a discussion about the annual party my husband and I are planning. It's quite a local institution. By the way, I'm Laura Hamilton. We've never met formally, but we have the place next to you. You know, the sheep.'

He nodded grimly, acknowledging the sheep which occasionally managed to scramble over the stone wall on to his own property.

'Anyway,' Laura rushed on, 'I'm so glad we ran into you.' She laughed nervously. 'Although not so literally, of course! It gives me a chance to invite you to the party. It's just local people. You know, before the tourists descend.'

While Laura chattered, Claudia stared straight ahead in an agony of embarrassment. The party was bad enough. Now Laura was actually inviting this man to it. It was too much! She'd just have to leave, go back to San Francisco, find a place of her own to live, get away from this place, this disturbing man. It had been a mistake to come here.

Then she noticed that there was a passenger in the truck. The door opened, and a tall, blonde woman got out. She descended gracefully to the pavement and, as she approached, Claudia couldn't take her eyes off her glowing beauty, the carefully arranged hair gleaming in the sunlight, the impeccable trouser-suit of pale blue linen, but most of all her erect, poised carriage.

She picked her way carefully through the broken glass directly to the man's side. Slipping an arm through his, she looked up at him with wide, greenish eyes. She seemed out of place in the rustic setting, more like a tourist than a native, and Claudia wondered who she could be. From her proprietorial air towards Julian Graves, it seemed she was a close friend of his.

Claudia was so engrossed in watching the blonde woman that she hadn't been listening to the conversation, but now her ears perked up when she heard Laura's next comment.

'Well, that's all settled then. We'll be expecting you. A week from Saturday. Eight o'clock. And of course,' she added with a gracious nod at his companion, 'the invitation extends to any friend you might care to bring along.' She settled back in her seat. 'Goodbye, then, Mr Graves. My husband will call you about the damage to your vehicle.'

Claudia waited until Julian Graves and his blonde companion were back in the truck and had driven away before she even dared to start the car again. Then she pulled slowly and cautiously into the wide space in front of the grocery store. When she was safely parked, the engine shut off, she turned to Laura and gave her a stony look.

'Did you have to invite him to the party?'

'Well, I thought it was a prudent thing to do, considering that we *did* hit him. Don't worry. I doubt if he'll come.'

'Didn't he accept your invitation?'

'He didn't decline or accept. He seems to be a man of very few words.'

They got out of the car and started walking towards the store. At the door, Claudia turned to her. 'Who was the blonde?'

Laura shrugged. 'I have no idea.' She pushed the door open and went inside. 'But,' she added over her shoulder, 'local gossip has it that she's not the only string to his bow. According to Mrs Jacobs, who cleans for him, too, he doesn't lack for female companionship.'

The next two weeks passed quickly, far too quickly for Claudia, who firmly pushed all thoughts of the dreaded party out of her mind whenever they intruded. This became increasingly difficult to do, however. With each passing day, Laura and Mrs Jacobs, and even Peter, became more deeply involved in plans and preparations for food, decorations, and even music, until in the end it was the sole topic of conversation in the Hamilton household.

Finally, Claudia made up her mind that her only recourse was simply to refuse to go. Just because she was living under her brother's roof, there was no law that said she had to, after all. They'd said it themselves: it was her home, too. She could do as she liked.

Besides, she had a good excuse. It had rained steadily for a solid week, and the damp always made her leg ache. She hadn't been to her garden once since the collision with Julian Graves. Even though they were in the habit of ignoring each other as they worked anyway, she couldn't bear the thought of seeing him again, much less risk another discussion of her driving prowess.

As it turned out, it was Laura herself who gave her the perfect opportunity to make her announcement on the Friday night before the party. They were just finishing dinner, and Laura was describing her new dress to Peter, who listened abstractedly, pretending an interest both his wife and sister knew quite well he didn't feel.

When she was through, she turned to Claudia. 'Have you decided yet what you're going to wear?'

Claudia laid her fork down carefully, pushing her plate away and took a deep breath. 'I'm not going to the party,' she said.

Peter's head came up sharply. 'Not going to the party? Don't be ridiculous. Of course you're going to the party!'

'No, Peter. I'm not. It's all decided.'

They glared silently at each other for several seconds in a silent battle of wills. Gradually, Peter's face grew red and his eyes bulged, sure signs of rising temper. Claudia steeled herself for battle. Then Peter opened his mouth. But, before he could blurt out what was on his mind, Laura rose abruptly to her feet and gave her husband a look full of meaning.

'Peter, would you mind leaving Claudia and me alone for a little while?'

His mouth snapped shut. His angry eyes darted from one to the other. Then, making a little noise of disgust deep in his throat, he got up, threw his napkin down on the table, and stalked out of the room without a backward glance.

When the back door has slammed behind him, Laura sat down and turned to Claudia. 'Now, I'm not going to nag you into doing anything you really don't want to do,' she said carefully. 'But I must tell you that I think you're making a big mistake to shut yourself up this way. You can't hide from reality for ever.'

'It's my leg,' Claudia said defensively. 'You know how badly it aches in this weather.'

Laura nodded. 'Yes, of course. I do know, and I sympathise.' She laid a hand on her arm. 'But Claudia, we're not asking you to do anything physically demanding. We only want you to put in an appearance. For our sakes, yes, but most of all for your own.'

'For my sake?' Claudia frowned. 'I don't understand.'

Laura leaned forward. 'Claudia, I'll never forget when you were a young girl, how tenacious you were about your dancing. You never gave up. How many times did you fall and fail during those gruelling practice sessions? And then always picked yourself up and tried again?'

'That was different,' Claudia replied heatedly. 'Dancing was my life.'

She looked away and gazed sullenly down at her plate as the tears of self-pity welled up behind her eyes.

'It was other things as well,' Laura persisted gently. 'Do you remember learning to swim? You half drowned several times, but always came back for more. I admired your courage and determination so much. And,' she added softly, 'that's why I hate seeing you turn into a coward now.'

Claudia turned on her angrily, ready to defend herself, but stopped short when she saw the unmistakable light of genuine love shining in the mild blue eyes. She bit her lip and looked away.

Laura was right, of course. It hurt to admit it, but she knew it was true. The only reason she was refusing to attend the party that meant so much to her brother and his wife was because she couldn't bear to face their friends, her old friends too, with her scarred leg, her hideous limp, her ruined career.

That still didn't mean she had to go, however, and she dredged up another excuse. 'I don't have anything to wear,' she muttered.

Laura smiled. 'Of course you do. There's a whole closetful of your old evening dresses up in your room.' She got up and held out a hand. 'Come on, let's go take a look. Surely we can find something, and we still have time to do some clever remodelling.

In the end, she'd given in, of course. Once again Laura's gentle persuasion had won out where Peter's heavy-handed anger had failed, and at half-past seven on Saturday night, with every nerve raw and her heart thudding painfully at the thought of the ordeal ahead, Claudia stood at the top of the stairs, ready to make her entrance.

She'd spent an agonising hour in front of the mirror in her bedroom getting ready, and now, still wondering how on earth she'd allowed herself to be talked into it, she smoothed down the folds of the long red velveteen dress, a dress she hadn't worn since college days, and made her way slowly down the stairs.

At the bottom landing, she heard voices and the sounds of crockery, pots and pans, cutlery coming from the kitchen, where all the activity seemed to be centred, and she limped slowly in that direction.

When she got there, she stood in the doorway for a moment, taking in the sight of Peter, resplendent in his best dinner-jacket, and Laura, radiant in her new pale blue silk. They were giving last-minute instructions to Mrs Jacobs, who was to stay and help serve the drinks and buffet supper.

'Well,' Claudia said as she stepped inside, 'what do you think?'

They all turned around at once, and three pairs of eyes fastened on her in sweeping, speechless appraisal. Finally, Peter's face broadened in a wide grin. He came over to her, put his hands on her shoulders and bent down to kiss her lightly on the cheek.

'That's my girl,' he murmured. 'You look beautiful, little sister.'

In the glow of the unmistakable pride in his eyes, Claudia felt herself relaxing, the frayed nerves receding. She glanced at Laura. 'Is the dress all right, then?'

Laura nodded with satisfaction. 'It's perfect. It was definitely a wise move to get that girlish flounce off the neckline. Now all you have to do is enjoy yourself.'

Claudia only nodded. All she had really agreed to was to put in a token appearance for the sake of her family, but that was as far as she was prepared to go.

After an hour or so, she could slip away quietly and that would be the end of that.

Just then, the front doorbell rang. Claudia put a hand to her throat and gave Laura a stricken glance. Laura only smiled, wiped her hands on a towel and turned to Peter.

'Sounds like our guests have started to arrive. Shall we go?'

While Peter and Laura went together to answer the door, Claudia hurried as fast as her leg allowed out to the terrace. Her intention was to remain firmly ensconced out there for a decent interval, and definitely seated, so as to avoid having to display her limp to the entire company.

As it turned out, however, once the guests started to arrive she actually began to enjoy herself. Laura and Mrs Jacobs had outdone themselves with hors-d'oeuvres, hot canapés and a sumptuous buffet of salads, cold cuts and a variety of home-baked breads. There was good music, good talk, and no one paid the slightest attention to her injured leg or referred once to the accident that had caused it.

Luckily, Jenny and her husband, Bill, were the first to arrive, which put her immediately at ease. Several of her other old schoolfriends had been invited, she knew, for her sake, and before she knew it, it was ten o'clock and her escape plans had been entirely forgotten.

She was sitting out on the terrace with Jenny when she saw him. At first she didn't recognise the strange man in the well fitting dark suit, the recently cut black hair and, above all, the smooth-shaven face. It wasn't until he came walking towards her and she looked up into the cool grey eyes that she realised it was Julian Graves.

The transformation in him was astounding, and for a moment all she could do was stare up at him in amazement. He was standing before her now, gazing down at her with a half amused sardonic smile on his long, lean face.

Her heart began to sink under that silent scrutiny, and a familiar load of depression threatened. She'd actually been enjoying herself until he showed up, she thought bitterly. The appreciative looks and sincere compliments on her appearance, the genuinely warm welcome she'd received from her old friends, all had made her feel attractive once again, even desirable.

Now it was all spoiled. If only she'd stuck to her original plan she would have been out of there by then, safe upstairs behind the locked door of her own bedroom. Now she'd have to wait until he left. She hoped his blonde was with him. At least that would keep him occupied and he'd leave her alone.

'Good evening, Claudia,' he said at last. He inclined his head slightly in Jenny's direction to include her, and she immediately jumped to her feet.

'Goodness,' she said, 'I haven't even seen Bill for hours! If I don't watch him, he'll eat everything in sight. And before Claudia could stop her, she'd hurried away from them towards the house.

When she'd disappeared inside, the tall man sat down easily in the chair she'd just vacated. He settled back, perfectly relaxed, his long legs stretched out before him, and took a swallow of his drink. Then he set it down on a nearby table and leaned towards her, his elbows resting on his knees.

'I hardly recognised you, Claudia,' he said in a low tone. 'That's a very becoming dress.'

Claudia flushed deeply as his gaze swept over her.

She was uncomfortably aware of the deeply scooped neckline, which was just short of being dangerously low since the ruffle had been removed. Then she wondered what she had to be ashamed of. At least she still had her dancer's figure, and her scarred leg was covered by the heavy folds of the red dress. Besides, who was Julian Graves to make her feel so awkward and ill at ease?

She gave him a distant smile. 'You've undergone a rather startling transformation of your own since the last time we met.'

He rubbed a hand over his face. 'You mean the beard?'

Somehow the gesture reminded her of the day he'd picked her up after she'd slipped on the wet grass. She could still feel the rasp of his heavy beard on her face, and found herself wondering how that smooth cheek would feel against hers now.

'It was only an experiment,' he said in an offhand tone. Then suddenly he smiled. 'Or chalk it up to sheer laziness. It kept me warm in the winter.'

Someone had put a slow tune on the stereo. The evening air was quite comfortable after an exceptionally fine day, and, as the music drifted outside, several couples started to dance their way out of the house on to the wide, paved terrace.

Julian raised a heavy enquiring eyebrow, then rose to his feet and came to stand before her. 'Would you care to dance?' he said, and reached out a hand.

Claudia shrank back instinctively. Her mouth was already open to decline, but when she looked up at him she stopped short. His dark head was outlined against the glow coming from inside the hose, and the coloured Japanese lanterns Peter had strung from the house across the terrace twinkled above him. The strong, sweet odour of lilac hung on the air, and suddenly she was tempted.

The music, the starry sky, the balmy, scented air, all created an intensely romantic setting that she found impossible to resist, in spite of all her firm intentions. Besides, it was a slow tune, the terrace was crowded now with dancing couples, and if she just shuffled her feet around in place, her limp would be disguised. He didn't seem like the kind of man who would execute intricate steps or immediately start throwing her around.

'All right,' she said, plunging ahead.

She braced a hand on the arm of her chair and stood up. Then, before taking one step, she leaned into his arms and they closed around her.

They hadn't danced for five seconds before she realised how thoroughly she had deceived herself. He was holding her loosely, with no real support, and there was no way she could conceal the hated limp, not when each step sent a shaft of excruciating pain up the whole length of her left leg. She bit her lip and looked away from him as the cold beads of perspiration broke out on her forehead.

'Is something wrong?' she heard him ask in a low voice.

She looked up at him. He was frowning faintly, his forehead creased, his eyes narrowed. She had to tell him. She'd been a fool to imagine she could deceive anyone, much less a sharp-eyed artist.

'It's my leg,' she murmured.

'Your leg? What's wrong with your leg?' Then the stern look faded and a light dawned in his eyes. 'Oh, you must mean the accident.'

She nodded miserably. 'Yes, you see . . .'

'Well, it *was* your fault,' he said easily. 'I can't be

blamed for your bad driving.' He drew her closer into his arms, holding her tightly against him, and laid his cheek against hers. 'But I can do my bit to help,' he breathed into her ear. 'Lean on me, Claudia. I'll hold you so you can take the weight off your leg.'

Claudia closed her eyes and sank mindlessly up against the broad chest. How could she tell him the truth now, when it felt so heavenly, so *safe*, to be within the circle of those strong arms, the long, lithe body pressed against hers?

With his strong arms supporting most of her weight, she virtually floated, her feet barely touching the ground. Little by little she gave herself up to the sheer pleasure of the moment, and her mind moved back in time until she'd almost convinced herself the accident last autumn never happened, that the past six months were only an unpleasant dream.

After a while a breeze came up, chilling the air, and she became dimly aware that the others had given up one by one and gone inside. She could still hear voices, laughter, music, coming from the house, but she knew she and Julian were alone on the terrace.

Suddenly she stopped in mid-step. She opened her eyes and looked up at him. His face was only inches away, hovering above her, his lips slightly parted, and an unmistakable light gleamed out of the wintry eyes. He still held her in a firm, close grip, and as his lips descended her only thought was to yield to the warmth spreading through her body, the fire singing in her bloodstream.

His mouth was cool and firm on hers. There was no forcing of his will in the kiss, no threat, no demand, no compulsion, only a gentle, tentative sliding motion that lulled her into total submission.

Gradually, imperceptibly, his lips began a more

penetrating exploration of her mouth, and the kiss deepened. At the same time, his hands encircled her waist, and his thumbs slid slowly up and down over her ribcage. Claudia held her breath, suddenly alert to danger. As though he could read her mind, he pulled back slightly, his hands stilled and he gazed down at her with hooded eyes.

'You're a very lovely creature, Claudia Hamilton,' he said in a low voice. 'I'd like to paint you one day.''

Claudia withdrew a hand from his shoulder and ran it over her smooth hair. The man enchanted her, mesmerised her with his uncanny ability to guage her reactions. The way he boldly pushed when he sensed her response, then backed off when she withdrew, had to mean only one thing. He'd had a lot of practice.

He put an arm around her and led her over to a nearby *chaise*, holding her just firmly enough to give her exactly the help she needed. The man was a wizard! She sank gratefully into the chair, exhausted from the physical and emotional effort of the past hour in his arms.

He stood over her, gazing down thoughtfully. Finally he said, 'Tomorrow I have to go out of town for a week or so. While I'm gone, I hope you'll give that leg plenty of rest. I want you to be a whole woman when I get back. There's a lot we can do together this summer, and I can't hold you up for ever.'

He smiled as he spoke, but there was an underlying ring of conviction to his words that made Claudia's blood run cold. A man like this one would naturally demand perfection in his women. She ought to tell him the truth now, before her imagination ran away with her and she started to build her hopes on a relationship with him.

But he didn't give her a chance. He bent down easily and took her face in his hands, his eyes burning into her as though he wanted to memorise every feature.

'It's late,' he said. 'And you're tired.'

He kissed her lightly on the lips, then straightened up and with one last look turned and strode into the house. Claudia watched him until he vanished from sight. When he was gone, cold reality descended on her, and she shivered in the cool night air. She knew without a doubt that he was walking out of her life.

CHAPTER THREE

CLAUDIA lay in bed that night, every muscle tense, in an agony of self-revulsion, and burning with shame. What had she done? What had possessed her to lie like that? Surely he'd have to learn the truth eventually. One word from Mrs Jacobs about that 'poor Hamilton girl' and it would all be over.

In the dark, deep recesses of her mind, however, she knew exactly why she had allowed him to believe her injury was only temporary, merely the result of that silly collision. From the moment he had come strolling out on to the terrace that evening, virtually glistening in his fine clothes and impeccable grooming, she'd wanted nothing more than to feel his strong arms around her, to lean against that broad chest, to pretend she was a whole, desirable woman again.

Well, she'd had her stolen moment. She could still feel the taste of his cool mouth on hers, the muscles of his arms and shoulders under her hands, the long legs propelling her around the terrace as they danced. It had been heaven, but nothing in this life was free, and now she'd have to pay for it.

She rolled painfully over on to her side and stared out the open window at the black night sky. She thought about the blonde she'd seen him with the day of the accident. Julian Graves would require that kind of perfection in his women and, when he found out her handicap was permanent, his ardour would be effectively dampened.

In the end, it probably wouldn't matter anyway. The man was obviously a predator and, while it had been a heady experience for her to be his prey for one night, her instinct told her that even if she'd been a whole woman there could never be a future for her with a man like Julian Graves. There had been the glint of desire in those cold grey eyes while he'd held her and kissed her, but not a scintilla of warmth, certainly no hint of genuine affection.

Each time they'd met, she'd sensed a simmering substratum of anger in the man, a near rage that seemed to be directed at her, perhaps at all women; and, while she found this quality in him oddly compelling, it also frightened her. He covered it well, too, with his smooth, practised charm. Only the eyes gave him away. They were like stones, and his rare smiles never warmed them.

She couldn't give him the chance to humiliate her. Her only hope of salvaging her pride was to avoid him. He said he'd be gone for a week. He probably wouldn't contact her again when he came back anyway, but, just in case he did intend to follow through his great seduction plans, she'd use that week to fortify herself against him.

On Monday she had another therapy session with Jenny, who was ecstatic about her progress.

'It's remarkable, Claudia,' she said as she eased the leg up and down, back and forth. 'You've exceeded my wildest expectations.'

Claudia, flat on her back, eyed her friend, who was still panting a little from her exertions. 'Do you mean it?'

'Of course I do.' She laughed. 'Surely you know by

now how ruthless I can be about telling you unpleasant truths.' She wiped her forehead with a towel, straightened up and held out a hand. 'I think that's enough for today. Come on. You can sit up now.'

Claudia took her hand, raised herself up and stretched both legs out in front of her, flexing the sore calf muscles. 'You know,' she said, 'I think you might be right. Every day it seems I can do more before it starts aching.'

Jenny was packing her equipment into her bag, towels, lotions, rubbing alcohol. She looked up at Claudia and gave her a knowing grin.

'Well, I certainly never thought I'd see you dancing again this soon,' she commented.

Claudia stared. 'Dancing?'

Jenny zipped up the bag. 'Sure. Don't tell me it's slipped your mind already. The party? Saturday night? The mysterious Julian Graves?'

Claudia reddened and stared down at her legs. 'Oh, that,' she muttered with a dismissive wave of her hand.

'Yes, that. I realise you were floating on a cloud out there, but you can't possibly have forgotten the whole episode. I haven't seen that certain look on your face since you made your début in San Francisco eight years ago.'

'Oh, Jenny, it was only a dance. It didn't mean anything.'

Jenny raised an eyebrow. 'No? Well, it didn't look that way to me. He was holding you so tight, I was afraid you'd melt together. And from the way he looked at you, I expected him to gobble you up right out there on the——'

'Jenny!' Claudia cried. 'Please! Stop it! I told you it

wasn't anything.'

Jenny cut off in mid-sentence, simply stared, her mouth wide open. The smile vanished, and she held out a tentative hand. 'Hey, what's wrong?' she said softly. 'What did I do? You know me. I was just kidding around. I didn't mean anything by it.'

Claudia couldn't meet her eyes. She slid off the table and gingerly tested her weight on the bad leg. She put on her robe and tied it loosely. Finally she turned to face her friend.

'I'm sorry, Jenny. I guess I over-reacted again. I shouldn't have yelled at you. But can't you see what it does to me when you even joke about it, even hint that there's some kind of—of—*romance*, for heaven's sake, brewing between me and a man like Julian Graves? It's a fairy-tale, not even worth discussing.'

Jenny gave her a puzzled look. 'Look, I don't understand. What's wrong with Julian Graves? I thought he looked absolutely devastating with those clothes, that haircut, the beard gone . . .'

'It's not him!' Claudia broke in angrily. She lifted her left leg a few painful inches and pointed at it. 'It's me! It's this awful leg, the disgusting limp.'

'Well, honey, I assume he saw that,' Jenny commented drily.

Claudia pulled her robe tighter. 'Oh, yes. He saw it. He just doesn't know it's permanent.'

'I see.' Jenny thought a moment, then shrugged. 'Well, in a sense it isn't—permanent, that is. I mean, your therapy is coming along so well that, in time, the limp will barely be noticeable.'

'And the scars?' Claudia said in a cold, steady voice. 'Will they go away in time, too?'

'Well, they'll fade. It's only been six months. And there's always plastic surgery.'

'I never want to go near a hospital again,' Claudia said with feeling. 'Besides, you know quite well I'll never dance again, no matter how much therapy or how many operations I have.'

Jenny put her hands on her hips and gave Claudia an exasperated look. 'Well, dancing and living—and loving, for that matter—aren't exactly the same thing, you know.'

Their eyes met and held. Then Claudia smiled crookedly. 'Aren't they? They are to me.'

'OK, OK,' Jenny said, raising her hands in the air. 'I give up. Have it your way.' She glanced at her watch. 'I've got to run now for my next appointment.'

They walked together silently down the long hall to the front of the house and outside on to the porch. The sun was directly overhead, and a gentle, salt-tanged breeze rustled the tall treetops surrounding the house. On the ground, the robins were busily poking their bills in Laura's perennial bed, searching for nesting material and littering the path with their discarded twigs and dead leaves.

Claudia walked with Jenny to her car and, when she was inside, she leaned down at the open window to speak to her.

'I'm sorry, Jenny,' she said softly, 'for being so beastly to you. You know how grateful I am for all you've done for me. Without you I'd still be using crutches or a cane, or even still be wearing that awful steel brace. It's just that it hasn't been easy to accept that my life as I knew it is over. I know you mean well, but it's cruel to raise my hopes that I can have a normal life again. It just makes it that much harder to face the truth again.'

'My dear girl,' Jenny said with a sigh, 'you simply must get that defeatist notion out of your head.

You've made wonderful progress.' She tilted her head to one side and gave Claudia a stern look. 'You know what I think?'

'No,' Claudia said with resignation. 'But I know you're going to tell me.'

Undaunted, Jenny ploughed on doggedly. 'I think you identified so powerfully and completely with your dancing that you've convinced yourself you can't have *any* kind of life without it. That's simply not true.'

Claudia gave her a sad smile. 'Oh, Jenny——' she began.

'No, let me finish. Whether you realise it or not, dancing is *not* all there is to life. You're only twenty-seven years old, you're an attractive woman. Why shouldn't a man love you? Bill loves *me*, for heaven's sake, and I don't have half your looks. You could marry, have children. You could even teach dancing.'

Claudia's face shut down at the mere mention of that. She knew there was no point in arguing any more. She backed away and they said goodbye. But, as she watched the little blue car disappear around the bend of the hill, she had to wonder if there might not be at least a grain of truth in Jenny's passionate lecture.

Was there hope? Hope for what? Immediately the picture flashed into her mind of a tall, dark man with cold, grey eyes, and she shivered a little in the bright sunlight. Then she shook her head, turned and started back up the path towards the house.

Just as she reached the porch, she heard the sound of another engine coming up the drive, definitely not Jenny's noisy Toyota. She turned around, shading her eyes with her hand against the sun.

She didn't recognise the dusty blue Volkswagen,

which looked as though it had had a lot of hard use recently. Her heart skipped a beat, then began to pound erratically. Could it be? He said he'd be gone a week. Somehow Jenny's argument made it all seem possible. Perhaps fairy-tales did sometimes come true. She'd tell him the truth, and maybe . . .

But it wasn't Julian. A stocky, sandy-haired man got out of the car and came walking towards her, a broad grin on his face. His arms opened wide as he approached her.

'Charles!' she cried. 'What a lovely surprise!'

She limped towards him as quickly as she could manage, and his arms came around her in a warm bear-hug. He put his hands on her narrow shoulders and kissed her lightly on the forehead.

'Claudia, you're looking marvellous, absolutely glowing.' He laughed. 'Much better than the last time I saw you, lying in that hospital bed six months ago.'

'Oh, yes,' she agreed happily. 'There's been a great improvement. But tell me, what in the world are you doing in Hidden Harbour?'

'Why, I came to see you, of course, among other things. You never did answer my letter.'

Claudia sobered instantly and looked away. 'No,' she said, 'I didn't.'

'Does that mean you're still considering the teaching job? As business manager of the dance company, I have *carte blanche* to offer you an enormous salary.' When she didn't say anything, he put an arm around her shoulders. 'They really want you, Claudia.'

She took a deep breath and turned to face him. 'Charles——' she began, then broke off.

'Look,' he said. 'I know it's too soon. You don't

have to make a decision now. Wait until the season starts in the autumn. I just want you to think about it.'

'I don't know, Charles. I'd pretty well made up my mind to decline the job. I just don't think I could bear to be around the company again, the dancers, knowing I'll never . . .'

He hugged her to him. 'No need to explain,' he said gruffly. 'I understand. Just give it time. OK?'

She forced a smile. 'OK.'

'That's my girl.'

As they started walking towards the house, Laura appeared on the front porch. When she saw Charles, she smiled delightedly and came running towards him, her hands outstretched in greeting.

'Charles Thornton!' she cried warmly. 'What a wonderful surprise.'

'Hello, Laura.' He took both her hands in his and leaned down to kiss her lightly on the cheek. 'You're looking as beautiful as ever.'

'Oh, go on with you!' she said, flushing with pleasure. 'Come inside. Let's go into the kitchen and I'll put on a fresh pot of coffee. Have you had lunch? You'll stay for dinner, won't you? Are your bags in the car? We have plenty of room. You can stay here as long as you like.'

'Hey, slow down,' Charles said with a laugh. 'You do know how to sweep a man off his feet, Laura.'

They were in the kitchen, warm and spicy-smelling. Claudia and Charles sat down at the round oak table by the window, while Laura put on a pot of coffee. Then she sniffed the air, opened the oven and poked her head inside.

'Good,' she said with satisfaction. 'I have some nice cinnamon rolls just about ready. Now, tell us what you're doing here and how long you can stay with us.'

'Well, first of all, I appreciate the offer, but I can't stay with you. Actually, I'm up here to meet some friends of mine who own a boat. Going to do some fishing up in the Canadian waters.'

'Oh, Charles!' Claudia teased. 'And I thought you came just to see me.'

'Well, I'll admit that did affect my decision, but we're leaving first thing in the morning and will spend tonight on the boat. It's moored down at the marina.'

'How long will you be gone?' she asked.

'The plan is to stay out two weeks.' He laughed. 'But I don't know if I'll be able to tolerate the cramped quarters with three other men for that length of time.'

'Will we see you when you get back?'

He laid a hand over hers, and looked directly into her eyes. 'You can count on it.' He glanced up at Laura, who was busy at the kitchen counter, humming under her breath and clattering crockery and silverware, then turned back to Claudia. 'You must know that neither the fishing trip nor the teaching job were the real reason I came, Claudia,' he said softly.

Laura turned suddenly and glanced quickly from one to the other. Then she said brusquely, 'I'm going to see if I can find Peter. I know he'll want to see you.'

She bustled out of the room, and when she was gone there was a short, awkward silence. Claudia didn't know what to say. Although she wasn't really totally shocked at the implication of his words, she was surprised that he would make such an open declaration. It had always been understood between them—between her and any man who was interested in her—that her single-minded dedication to dancing always came first.

But now everything was changed, and she looked at him with new eyes. Maybe Jenny was right, after all. Maybe there *was* a life for her. At least this man wanted her. But did she want him?

'Charles,' she said at last, 'I don't know what to say.'

He reached out and put a finger over her mouth. 'No,' he said. 'Don't say anything. I wanted to see you before I went out on the boat, just to plant a seed, so to speak. Think about it while I'm gone. Then, when I come back—well,' he shrugged, 'we'll see.'

Then the sound of voices came from the hallway, and Laura came back inside, followed by a beaming Peter, his hand outstretched to Charles in greeting. Laura poured out the coffee while the two men chatted, then came over to the table, her arms laden with a tray full of steaming coffee mugs and a plate of hot rolls. She glanced briefly from Charles to Claudia, then set the tray down and smiled.

'Well, come on. Let's tuck in.'

During the next week, Claudia did think about it, almost constantly. The trouble was that every time she formed a picture of Charles in her mind another face intruded, and, as hard as she tried, she simply couldn't keep her mind focused on her old friend.

She knew it was foolish to give even a passing thought to Julian, and she kept remindingherself that she had quite firmly made up her mind the night of the party that she couldn't afford the risk of getting involved with him. Even if he could tolerate her limp, her scars, she knew in the depths of her being that there was no future with him. The anger in him went too deep. He was a loner, a cold, aloof solitary, who might want to play with her for a while, but that would be all.

Charles, on the other hand, would probably want to marry her eventually. He would take care of her, protect her, made her safe. He was that kind of man.

As the days passed, her conviction only strengthened. On the following Saturday, when the week he'd said he'd be gone was over, not only had he not appeared, but there was no word from him, nor any sign that he had come back to Hidden Harbour.

She went down to her garden plot every day, wondering if he'd be working in the field next door, but it was always empty. She was even tempted once to ask Mrs Jacobs about him when she came to clean, but the woman was such a terrible gossip she didn't dare. As she'd told Jenny, it was only a fairy-tale anyway. She'd just have to write off Julian Graves.

Two weeks later to the day, and true to his word, Charles did return from his fishing trip. He had called her twice from the boat on the ship-to-shore radio, and had arranged to come directly out to the house as soon as they docked that evening.

Late that afternoon, while she was up in her room getting ready, Claudia was gripped with a sudden panic. What was she going to tell him? He'd want an answer to his unspoken question. Did she want to encourage him?

She was tempted. It would be so safe. Since she couldn't have the dancing career she really wanted anyway, she could do a lot worse than marry Charles. Then she had to laugh. He hadn't even asked her yet! The next move was up to him, and for now she wouldn't discourage or encourage him.

When he arrived, tanned and fit from his holiday on the water, Laura immediately bustled him into the kitchen, where Peter was waiting for him with a cold beer. 'Now, I don't want any argument about this, Charles,' she said firmly. 'You're going to stay here with us for as long as you like. We have plenty of room.'

Charles shrugged his shoulders. 'Thanks, Laura,' he said with a quick, rueful glance at Claudia. 'But I can't. I just got a quick SOS this morning on the boat from my assistant. There's a big flap going on down in San Francisco over the scenery for our new production of *Swan Lake*. It seems the carpenters have just about decided to go out on strike.'

'Oh, no!' Claudia said with genuine sympathy. 'What timing!'

'Right,' he agreed grimly. 'It's just about perfect, too late to change our schedule. So, unless we want to open on a bare stage, I've got to get down there and see if I can put out a few fires.'

'When do you have to go?' Peter asked. 'Surely you can stay the night?'

Charles shook his head. 'Sorry, Peter. I'd love to, but I've already promised I'd leave tonight. The next ferry to the mainland leaves in half an hour, in fact. If I drive straight through, I should reach San Francisco some time tomorrow afternoon.'

He drained his beer, rose to his feet, and stood there awkwardly for a few moments. Then he gave Claudia a brief, questioning glance, and she realised he wanted to talk to her alone. She pushed her chair back and got up.

'I'll walk out to the car with you,' she said.

At the same time, Peter shuffled his own chair and half rose out of it, as though to join her, but his wife put a restraining hand on his arm. He gave her a puzzled look but, when she frowned slightly and shook her head, he settled back down.

'Well, if you can come back,' he said to Charles, 'you're always welcome here.'

After the two men had shaken hands and Charles had given Laura a goodbye peck on the cheek, Claudia walked with him down the hall and outside, where his car was parked in front. It was early evening, not quite seven o'clock. With daylight-saving time, the sun was just now beginning to sink below the western horizon, casting long, reddish streaks across the entire blue canopy of the sky.

He opened the car door, but before getting inside he turned to Claudia. 'I didn't plan to end my trip like this,' he said unhappily. 'Rushing off the minute I got back. I'd been looking forward to spending some time with you.'

'It's not your fault, Charles. You can't help it if you're so indispensable to the company.'

He laughed drily. 'Well, apparently I've got them fooled, anyway.' He reached out to take her hand, and his face softened. 'There are several things you and I need to talk about.'

'Charles——' she began warily.

'Don't,' he said. 'Don't say anything. I'm not going to push you, not about the teaching job—or anything else. All I ask is that you think about it. And me.'

She smiled at him and squeezed his hand. 'Yes,' she promised. 'I'll do that.'

'Good.' He put his arms around her and held her

close for a few moments. Then he turned his head to kiss her lightly on the mouth.

She felt so safe with Charles, so comfortable and secure with his arms around her. His lips were cool and dry. There was no demand there, only a steady, protective love. Perhaps, she thought, warming to him——

Just then, she heard the smooth, purring sound of a car coming up the drive. They broke apart, and Claudia looked up to see a strange car, an expensive-looking foreign model, which came to a stop not twenty feet away from them. The driver's window was rolled down, and Claudia instantly recognised the dark head of Julian Graves.

He *had* come back! A fluttering sensation started in her stomach and moved from her midsection up into her heart as she stared at him. Their eyes met, and she quickly looked back up at Charles.

'Who's your visitor?' he asked.

'Just a neighbour,' she murmured. Somehow, she didn't want the two men to meet.

He nodded and bent down to give her a last quick kiss. Then he got inside the car and started the motor. 'I'll call you when I get home,' he said.

He backed up and, with one brief wave, started down the hill. Claudia looked after him until he was gone. Then, almost against her will, she turned around to face Julian.

He was outside now, leaning back against the car, his arms crossed in front of him, his long legs spread apart, looking as though he owned the whole island. He was dressed neatly but casually in a pair of well fitting grey chinos and a darker grey knit shirt. His thin mouth was curled in an amused, sardonic smile, the heavy black eyebrows lifted slightly.

He pushed himself away from the car, shoved his hands in his trouser pockets and came ambling slowly towards her.

Claudia stood rooted to the spot, afraid to move, not only because she desperately didn't want him to see the limp that he expected to be gone by now, but because she didn't think she was capable of taking a step.

As she watched him approach, she felt the same sense of impending danger from him that she always did, but with the same irresistible pull of senseless attraction. In that split second, she mentally compared the two men and almost laughed aloud at the contrast between them. There was no comfort, no safety in this tall dark stranger, only a threat to her hard-won, precarious peace of mind.

He stood before her now, so tall that she had to crane her neck to look up at him. He made no move to touch her. Their eyes met and his smile broadened.

'Hello, Claudia,' he said. 'I've come back.'

'So I see.' She tried to make her voice light, but it only seemed to come out shaky.

'I came to take you to dinner.'

She bridled at that. No word from him for two weeks, then he marched back into her life, just assuming she'd drop everything to go out to dinner with him at the last minute. Before she could open her mouth to decline, however, he continued speaking.

'But perhaps you have other plans,' he said easily. He glanced down the drive in the direction Charles's blue Volkswagen had just taken. 'I'm sorry if I interrupted something important. I should have called first.'

The courteous tone completely disarmed her and,

as her irritation faded, she realised she wanted very much to go out to dinner with him. Why not? What harm would it do? If he backed off when he noticed she still had her limp, what did it really matter? Somehow, knowing Charles wanted her in spite of her handicap had given an enormous boost to her confidence and morale. And Julian *had* come back.

'I'll have to change,' she said.

'Why? You look fine the way you are.' His eyes travelled over the thin, cream-coloured silk blouse and brown linen slacks. 'The island doesn't offer much in the way of exotic cuisine, anyway,' he added drily. 'In fact, Martha's Kitchen is probably the only place open this early in the season.'

Laura appeared on the porch just then. 'Oh, has Charles gone already?' she called.

'Yes,' Claudia replied. 'He had to catch his ferry.'

'Too bad. I wanted to say goodbye.'

Claudia laughed. 'You already did that.'

Laura's gaze shifted to the tall man. 'Hello, Julian,' she said politely.

Julian nodded. 'Laura.'

There was a short, awkward silence. Julian glanced down at Claudia, still standing immobile beside him, and raised his eyebrows quizzically. It was up to her, the look said.

'Julian and I are going down to the village to have a bite to eat,' she said at last.

Laura's eyes widened. 'Oh,' she said. Then she smiled. 'Well, have a good time,' and turned and went back inside.

When she was gone, Julian put a hand lightly under Claudia's elbow. 'Shall we?'

Well, here goes, she thought. She drew in a deep breath and took the first awkward step.

It wasn't so bad, she decided, as they walked along. The limp was still noticeable, of course, but at least she didn't have to drag the foot behind her like a dead weight, the way she had at first. Jenny was right. There was a big improvement.

At the car, he stopped and put his hand on the door, but before opening it, he stood still and frowned at her.

'You're still limping,' he said.

'Yes. But it's much better.'

He opened the door and she got inside, praying that he'd drop the subject. But when he was settled behind the wheel, he turned to her, still frowning.

'I can't imagine why your leg hasn't healed completely by now,' he said in a puzzled voice. 'It wasn't that bad a collision. Shouldn't you have it looked at?'

Now, she thought. Now is the time to tell him the truth. She looked at him. He was so close to her that she could see the faint, dark bristles of his beard on his face, smell the scent of clean soap and fresh outdoors. The breeze coming through his window had tousled his dark hair so that one lock had fallen over his forehead, giving him a boyish look that softened the hard features.

Then she looked into his eyes. There was nothing soft in those smooth chunks of granite, and her precarious courage failed her. She looked away.

'Oh, I've seen a doctor. He says it will just take time.'

He shrugged then, apparently satisfied, and fired the engine. 'If you say so,' he said, and they started down the drive.

At the main road, he turned left to go into the village along the cliff road. The sun had gone down all the way by now, and the sky was only dimly lit by the afterglow. Dusk fell quickly in the islands. Soon it would be dark. She wished she's brought a sweater, and shivered a little in the cool breeze.

'Cold?' Julian asked.

She nodded. 'A little.'

He rolled up his window. 'That better?'

'Yes, fine. Thank you.'

A few minutes later he'd pulled up in front of Martha's, the one restaurant on the island that stayed open all year around. It was a popular gathering place for the local people in the off-season, but would be filled with tourists in a few weeks, when the boaters came north.

There were no street-lights in Hidden Harbour, so when Julian had shut off the engine and turned to her, his features were barely discernible in the pale glow cast by the lights from inside the restaurant. He made no move to get out of the car.

'You're a dancer, aren't you?' he asked at last.

'Yes. Yes, I am. How did you know that?'

He laughed. 'Certainly not from the way you move—or drive!'

Then the light dawned. 'Oh, I know,' she said grimly. 'Mrs Jacobs cleans for you, too, doesn't she?'

He expelled an impatient sigh. 'Believe me,' he said fervently, 'Mrs Jacobs and I have no conversation whatsoever. I learned that early on. She has strict orders never, under any circumstances, to pass along one item of local gossip.' He shook his head. 'The woman is a menace.' Then his voice gentled. 'I saw you dance once a few years ago in Los Angeles.'

She stared at him in the dimness. 'And you recognised me?'

'No, not right away.' He laughed. 'Especially not

after I saw you trip that day up in the field! It was when you hit my truck. I heard Laura call you by name, and the pieces fell into place.'

Now, she thought. Tell him now. Her hands twisted in her lap, and she opened her mouth to speak but, before she could get a word out, he had moved closer to her and reached out a hand to touch her hair.

'But I think I would have known anyway,' he said in a low, husky voice. 'I'll never forget that night I saw you dance. I was absolutely entranced. You were so graceful, so lovely.'

Hot tears stung behind her eyelids at this painful reminder of her past triumphs. She had to tell him, had to stop this right now, before she became more deeply enmeshed in deception.

But when his hand moved down, warm and soft, over her face, her chin, she couldn't speak. He grasped her lightly around the neck, then with his thumbs traced the high ridge of her collarbone under the thin opening of her blouse.

She couldn't move. The long, sensitive fingers gliding over her skin had set up a clamouring in her bloodstream, and a slow warmth began to spread throughout her whole body. She watched, transfixed, as his face descended, and when his mouth met hers her head began to whirl crazily as pure sensation obliterated all thought.

His lips parted slightly, and she felt the tip of his tongue gently probing. The hand at her throat moved slowly downwards, and when its warm pressure settled over her breast, she felt as though she was drowning in a pool of sheer pleasure, awash in a sensuous sea that was uncannily similar to what she'd experienced when she used to perform in front of an audience.

Then, abruptly, he broke the kiss. He pulled his head back and removed his hand. 'We'd better get inside,' he said hoarsely. 'Or else forget dinner altogether.'

The spell was broken. Without waiting for a reply, he opened his door and got out. As he came around the front to her side, he passed under the flickering neon light at the entrance, and Claudia stared as his fine features were briefly illuminated.

Oh, God, she thought, what's happening to me? She put a hand on her mouth where his lips had so recently pressed against it. What is it about this man?

CHAPTER FOUR

'THE reason I was late getting back to Hidden Harbour was that I stopped off in San Francisco to pick up my daughter.'

Claudia stared at him, her fork half-way to her mouth. 'Your daughter?' she said weakly.

'Yes. Her name is Margaret. She lives with my sister and her husband during the school year, but I keep her every summer.'

Claudia was stunned. This was the first she'd heard about a daughter. Why hadn't anyone known about her? Jenny had mentioned a dead wife, but nothing about a child.

'How old is she?' she asked when she found her voice.

'She's eight.' He swallowed the last of his lamb stew, wiped his mouth with his napkin and set it down on the table.

'What's she like?' Claudia asked.

He leaned back in the wooden booth and gazed at her with an appreciative gleam in his grey eyes. 'She's a lot like you, as a matter of fact. Oh, different colouring—she's quite fair—but the same fragile bone structure and narrow frame.'

Claudia flushed under that unblinking appraisal. The heat began to build in her again as she recalled their recent encounter in the car.

'In fact,' he went on with a smile, 'she wants to be a dancer herself. Or thinks she does. Perhaps you can give her a few pointers.'

'Perhaps,' she murmured. She pushed the food around on her plate, her appetite gone. A daughter? Who wanted to be a dancer? Finally she gave up on her dinner. She laid her fork down on her plate and eyed his dark good looks carefully.

'If your daughter is fair,' she said, 'then she must be like your wife.'

The pleasant smile vanished immediately, and the cold eyes hardened. Slowly, he took a packet of cigarettes out of his shirt pocket. Without offering one to her, he took one out, lit up, and dropped the spent match in the small glass ashtray, all in precise, deliberate movements.

He smoked silently for several seconds, his gaze fastened intently on the swirling grey smoke that rose above him. Just the colour of his eyes, Claudia thought. She realised she'd just made a terrible *faux pas*, but wasn't quite sure how. Surely, if he had a daughter, there had to have been a wife in the picture? Jenny herself had said she'd nursed her in her last illness.

Finally, he stubbed out his cigarette, shifted his weight and started to slide out of the booth. 'Are you through?' he asked, glancing at her half-full plate. 'You haven't eaten much.'

'Yes,' she said. 'I'm through.'

As she watched him pay the bill at the cash register near the front entrance, Claudia could hardly believe this stony-faced man was the same one who had kissed her so gently only an hour ago. He had frozen her out as completely as though they had suddenly inhabited different planets.

They walked in silence out to the car. It was pitch dark by now, and very quiet, except for the crashing of the waves against the rocks below and the low rustle of the tall fir trees that surrounded the high promontory.

The evening was effectively ruined, she thought, as he started the car and backed around. Apparently she'd trodden on a sore spot, ventured into forbidden territory with her question about his wife. But how was she to know? It was an innocuous question, and perfectly reasonable. From the quick, efficient way he handled the car, it looked as though he intended to drive her home as fast as he could, drop her off, and get out of her life for good.

She was surprised, then, when they reached the main road and, instead of turning towards her brother's ranch, he made an abrupt right and headed in the opposite direction. She sat quietly, her hands folded in her lap, and after a few minutes he turned to her.

'It's still early,' he said in a normal conversational tone. 'I thought we might take a drive around the island.'

No explanation, no apology, she thought with rising irritation. Not even a request or the remotest interest in what *her* wishes might be. Clearly, whatever was going to be between them would have to be on his terms, and she wasn't at all sure she liked his rules.

She glanced over at him. He had turned back to the road again so that his profile was etched in a sharp outline against the reflection of the headlights on the pavement, and she drew in a quick silent breath. The sheer beauty of the man pierced the hidden corners of her heart, and she longed to reach out and touch him, to smooth away the troubled lines on his forehead.

'That would be nice,' was all she said, and he drove on.

They drove past the marina, where a few boats, owned by the locals, were moored, their tall masts looming black against the dark sky, and after a few miles, the road descended sharply towards the beach. Julian slowed and pulled into a narrow dirt road that led directly to the one level strip of sand on the island, a public beach that was deserted now.

He cut off the engine, pulled on the handbrake, then turned to her. 'I'd like to get out and stretch for a minute. Would it be too chilly for you?'

'No, I don't think so.'

They got out and walked silently together for a few feet until they stepped on to a grassy verge at the edge of the gently sloping sandy beach. A pale moon had appeared in the sky, and the first bright evening star glittered overhead. From the shore came the gentle lapping of the waves as the tide receded, much more quietly here than on the rockier sections of the coastline.

They stood together for several moments without speaking or touching, until finally he turned and gazed down at her in the moonlight. She slowly raised her face to his, and as their eyes met it seemed to Claudia that a strange, hypnotic spell had been cast over them. She couldn't move, could scarcely breathe. She only waited, held inexorably by that piercing, searching gaze.

Julian didn't say a word. His head bent slowly towards her. She closed her eyes, waiting, until at last his lips met hers. She sank against him as his arms came around her, giving herself up totally to the magic of the moment, the sweetness of his kiss, the mobile mouth moving softly and sensuously against her own.

Suddenly, the pent-up tension she sensed in him seemed to explode. His arms tightened on her in a punishing grip, his lips opened wide, and his tongue thrust inside her mouth, probing, demanding. He pulled her roughly all along his lean, muscular frame, grinding her lower body against his taut, hard thighs.

He tore his lips from her mouth and placed them on her throat, forcing her head back until she was dangerously close to falling, but for the strong arm that held her around the waist. Her blood was on fire, her head buzzing, and she heard herself moan aloud as his mouth moved downwards and she felt his free hand come up to press against her breast.

His hands were fumbling with the buttons on her blouse now. She wanted to help him, but was frozen into weak immobility by the intensity of her response to his lovemaking. Underneath her blouse she wore only a sheer silk camisole. Like most dancers, she had small, firm breasts that never needed support, and as his warm, large hand moved over the thin material, sliding over the taut peaks, she could hardly breathe.

Still in a frenzy, his breath coming in rasps, he pulled her blouse off down her arms and slipped the straps of the camisole over her shoulders. His hand moved back and forth feverishly over her bare breasts for a moment, then he lowered his head and she felt his lips and tongue moving slowly, tantalisingly, up and down against the sensitive skin in a rhythmic motion that made her cry out with joy.

Then, in one swift movement, he straightened up and tore off his knit shirt, throwing it on the grass beside her blouse. He took her by the shoulders and pulled her up against his bare, broad chest, so that the tips of her breasts brushed lightly against the smooth, silky hair running down the centre of it.

By now she was limp with longing, mindless in her unbridled reaction to this man's magical lovemaking. He seemed much calmer now, gentler, as though he'd made an effort to control the animal passion that had seized him earlier, a passion she would never have dreamed simmered below his cool façade.

Still breathing hard, he looked down at her. His hands moved from her shoulders to travel gently over her bare breasts, outlining their shape with long, delicate strokes, brushing lightly over the aroused peaks, his eyes following his every movement.

With his hands still moving over her, he spoke at last. 'I'd love to paint you this way,' he breathed. He smiled crookedly and met her eyes. 'Would it embarrass you to pose nude for me?'

'I—I——' she croaked. She cleared her throat. 'No,' she said huskily. 'At least, I don't think so.'

It wasn't until his hands moved down to the fastening of her slacks that she remembered about her scarred leg. He had it undone now and was tugging the waistband over her hips before she found the presence of mind to stop him. She put her hand over his.

'No,' she said. 'Please. I'll be too cold.'

His hands stilled. He pulled back slightly and stared off into the distance for a moment, a dazed expression on his face. She crossed her arms over her breasts, shivering a little now that he had left her. Then he shook himself, ran a hand over his dark head, and looked into her eyes.

'God, Claudia, I'm sorry. Forgive me.'

He reached down and picked up their discarded clothing, still lying on the grass where it had fallen earlier. Carefully, he put her arms through the sleeves of her blouse and pulled it closed in front of her. He handed her the jacket, then turned and slipped his shirt over his head while she hastily buttoned her blouse.

'Julian——' she said when he was facing her again.

'Don't,' he said. 'Don't say anything. It was wonderful. I don't want to spoil it. I hope I *haven't* spoiled it.' He shook his head ruefully. 'I'm not like this ordinarily. I mean, I'm not a monk by any means, but I usually have myself under much better control and don't react quite so—so voraciously. I hope you believe that, Claudia.'

She could very well belive it. She'd been astounded herself at the explosive passion that lay beneath the controlled and rather ironic exterior he presented to the world. And *she* had been the one to arouse it in him! she thought with a warm inner glow.

She put a hand on his arm. 'I know,' she said softly. 'I felt it, too.' She laughed lightly and tucked her loose strand of hair behind her ear. 'I've never been quite so carried away myself. In fact, it's a lot like how I feel when I'm dancing, the exhilaration, the excitement . . .' She broke off and lowered her eyes, knowing she'd said too much.

'I can understand that,' he said gravely. 'When my painting is really going well, I feel much the same way.' He put an arm loosely around her shoulders. 'Come on. We'd better go.'

They drove along over the narrow road back through the darkened village towards the ranch, her head resting on his broad shoulder, his arm around her. She hadn't felt so happy since her accident. No, she amended, in her whole life, even before the accident. She'd compared her sensations in his arms to dancing, but this was much more real, more compelling. How ironic, she thought, that the terrible handicap that she was sure had ruined her life had ended by bringing her even greater joy.

She glanced over at him. As if sensing her eyes upon him, he tightened his hold on her, and she curled against him. She put out a hand and traced the clean line of his profile, from the dark hair over his forehead, down the straight, aristocractic nose, the fine mouth and firm chin.

There was no doubt in her mind now. She was totally, helplessly in love with him. And if he was still grieving for his dead wife, she would help him to forget. Of course he hadn't lived like a monk since her death. A man as attractive to women as he was couldn't possibly be celibate. She remembered quite well the lovely blonde woman who'd been with him the day of the accident. But *she* was the one who had broken through the barrier of his reserve.

As they made their way slowly up the drive to the house, her heart began to thud dully in anticipation of what lay ahead. She moved away from him and braced herself. She had to tell him now. There was no escape. What had happened tonight between them had seared her very soul. Lies and deception simply would not do. There was no room for them now. They had to start on a clean slate and, if he cared half as much for her as she did for him, he would understand.

He parked in front of the house and turned to her. 'Well,' he said, 'it's been quite an evening.' He reached out and put a hand on her face, then bent to kiss her lightly on the mouth. 'I'll call you tomorrow. I'd like to have you see my house, my studio, meet my daughter.'

She looked away, frowning with the struggle to

find the right words. He sat very still beside her, waiting silently for her reply.

'What's wrong?' he asked at last.

'Julian,' she said evenly. 'There's something I've got to tell you.'

'Oh, God, you're married?'

'No.'

'Engaged?'

'No.'

'Well, what then?'

She bit her lip. 'It's about my leg, my limp.'

'What about it? Listen,' he said with a laugh, 'don't get any bright ideas about suing me. Remember the collision was your fault. There were witnesses.'

She took a deep breath. 'I didn't hurt my leg in the collision.'

He gave her a puzzled look. 'No? How, then?'

'And it's not temporary.' She searched his face. 'Six months ago I was in a car accident in San Francisco. A woman was driving the other car. She'd been drinking. She turned left against a red light and hit me head-on. My left leg was crushed.'

She stopped. He had turned away from her and was gazing stonily out of the front window. In the light from the porch she could see a pulse working along his jaw. His lips were compressed in a firm line, his eyes narrowed into slits.

A feeling of dread began to gnaw in the pit of her stomach as she recognised all the old anger in him rising to the surface. He wasn't reacting at all as she had anticipated. He had withdrawn from her, back into his shell, and she hadn't a clue as to what was going through his mind, except that it wasn't good.

'Go on,' he said, without turning around.

She shrugged helplessly. It was too late to turn

back now. 'I spent weeks in a hospital having surgery to repair the damage to my leg, then months in a steel brace. I've had intensive therapy, and am told it will continue to improve until I barely limp at all. But,' she went on dully, 'I'll never dance again.'

He turned on her then. 'Why didn't you tell me this sooner?' he asked in a cold, clipped tone. 'Why wait until after you'd got my defences down and aroused my interest? And after I'd made such callow love to you?' he added in a sneering tone of contempt.

'I don't know. I certainly didn't plan to deceive you. I mean, it isn't something I like to talk about. I had no idea we would end up, well, like we did tonight.' She smiled weakly. 'How was I to know you'd sweep my off my feet?'

When he didn't respond, she flicked him a quick, furtive glance. His stern features were set in stone, and he was gripping the steering wheel so tightly his knuckles stood out. A cold fear gripped her, and something seemed to shrivel inside her.

Without another word, he got out of the car and came around to open the door for her. As they walked together up to the front porch, she was more excrutiatingly aware of her limp that she'd ever been before, even when it was at its worst, and she had the feeling he was too. There was simply nothing she could do to hide it, so she ploughed doggedly ahead until they reached the door.

Laura and Peter always left the door unlocked during the off-season, so she didn't need a key. She turned the knob, then hesitated. She looked up at him. He was staring off into the distance, as though his mind were a million miles away and she wasn't even there.

'All right, then?' he asked abruptly. He pushed the

door open, and she stepped inside.

'Julian . . .' she began, and turned around to face him once again, to plead for his understanding.

But all she saw was his tall form as he hurried away from the house and got inside the car. She closed the door and leaned back against it. The engine started, and she heard the sound of tyres squealing on the tarmac as he burned rubber getting out of there as fast as he could.

He didn't call her the next day as he'd said he would. Nor the day after that. At first she told herself she had to give him time. Her revelation about the extent of her injury had shocked him. He'd been attracted to a dancer, not a cripple, and it would take him time to adjust to that fact.

But as the days lengthened into a week, then two weeks, she knew he wasn't going to call at all. She tried to hide her grief from Laura and Peter and Jenny, but they all knew something was troubling her. How could they help it when all she did was mope around the house all day? She was simply helpless against the load of misery on her heart. It was bad enough before she'd fallen in love with Julian Graves. Now it was impossible.

Sharp-eyed Jenny, of course, was the first to confront her with it. It was at the fourth therapy session after that awful night, and when they'd finished for the morning she stood back from the table, put her hands on her hips and stared down at Claudia with a look of profound distaste.

'All right,' she said. 'What's going on?'

'Nothing's going on,' Claudia mumbled, and turned her head towards the wall so she wouldn't have to face those accusing brown eyes.

'Look at me, Claudia!' Astounded at the harshness in Jenny's voice, Claudia looked at her. 'Now,' Jenny went on in a gentler tone. 'Will you please tell me what's the matter, what's *been* the matter for the past two weeks? I don't understand you. You were making such brilliant progress, then all of a sudden you just quit. It's as though you've given up all over again. Now you've got to tell me what's wrong or I can't help you.'

Claudia closed her eyes. 'Jenny,' she said wearily, 'just back off, will you, please?' She put a hand over her forehead. 'I don't want to talk about it.'

Jenny didn't say anything for a long time. Finally Claudia could hear footsteps moving away, the familiar sound of Jenny packing up her things, then coming back to the table. Although Claudia kept her eyes averted, she could sense the long, penetrating stare boring into her.

'I'm leaving now, Claudia,' Jenny said finally. 'And I'm not coming back, at least not until you prove to me you're going to follow my instructions and at least *try* to get better.' She waited, but Claudia wouldn't even look at her. Then Jenny heaved a deep sigh. 'I can't do it for you, you know,' she went on. 'If you don't care, the best tharapist in the world can't help you.'

Claudia lay there, her eyes shut tight, the hot tears smarting behind her eyelids, and listened as Jenny slowly walked out of the room, her footsteps fading as she went down the hall, then the low murmur of voices as she conferred with Laura.

They're talking about me, Claudia thought resentfully. She opened her eyes and stared at the ceiling, allowing the tears to flow freely down her face. She knew she was wrong, a burden on everybody who loved her. Both Peter and Laura had been giving her strange, sidelong glances lately. They probably wanted to get rid of her. She didn't blame them.

Finally, she heard the front door close and the sound of Jenny's Toyota as it chugged down the drive towards the main road. She rolled over on her side with a groan. She'd have to leave. It was senseless to punish everyone else just because her heart was broken.

In a few minutes Laura came to her, and Claudia tensed up for another battle, hardening herself against a new onslaught of wholly justifed recriminations and accusations from her sister-in-law.

'Jenny says she's not coming back,' Laura said quietly.

'I know,' Claudia choked out in a strangled voice.

Laura came over to the table and put a hand on her shoulder. Claudia flinched away from it and, with a sigh, the hand was withdrawn. Neither of them said anything for a few minutes. Then Laura spoke again, this time in a hard voice that was totally unlike her.

'Tell me, Claudia, is he really worth it?'

Shocked at the cold tone, the pointed question, Claudia twisted around to face her. 'What do you mean?' she blurted out.

Laura smiled sadly. 'I'm not blind, Claudia. Ever since that night you went out to dinner with Julian Graves, you've gone downhill. You're not eating, you're getting no exercise at all, and Jenny just told me that if you keep on this way you'll be back in that steel brace again, possibly for good.'

'Jenny talks too much,' was the bitter reply. But the words stung, and her heart sank at the thought of having to wear the hated brace again.

'Jenny loves you!' Laura said sharply. 'We all do. Darling, you must pull yourself together. Can't you tell me what happened? It might help.'

At that, Claudia groaned and leaned into Laura's arms, sobbing out all the pain she'd been bottling up for the past two weeks. Laura patted her gently as she cried, making soothing noises, until finally it was over and she lifted her tear-stained face.

'I thought he cared about me,' she said. 'He said he'd call me the next day. I was so happy.'

'Well, darling, some men are like that.' Laura pursed her lips in a disapproving line. 'Especially men like Julian Graves, who are too attractive for their own good. Seduction and betrayal, I believe it's called,' she added in a dry tone.

'Oh, Laura,' Claudia groaned, 'you don't understand. He would have called, I know it. The best actor in the world couldn't have put on such a convincing performance. I know he was attracted to me as much as I was to him, until . . .'

'Until what?' Laura prompted.

Claudia stared dully at her. 'Until I told him about the accident, that I was permanently crippled, would never dance again. Then he just froze me out. I knew it was over. But why? That's what I don't understand. Is it so terrible? Am I so ugly?'

'Of course not!' Laura replied heatedly. 'You're a beautiful girl, a girl any man would be proud to love. He's the one who's crippled, not you. At the rate you were going, you would have ended up with hardly any limp at all. Jenny said so herself. So did the doctors. And if the man wanted you only because you were a famous dancer, then I say you're well rid of him. Who is he, after all, to make such demands on a woman? A mere painter!'

Claudia had to smile at the indignant tone. She sniffled twice, wiped her eyes on the back of her hand, then reached into the pocket of her robe to pull out a tissue and blew her nose. She heaved a deep sigh and moved her legs to dangle them over the edge of the table. Laura helped her down, and they walked together down the hall towards the kitchen, where something smelled very good.

'Now,' Laura said, 'I have a fresh pot of coffee brewing, and some of your favourite orange rolls ready to take out of the oven. You'll see, in time, you'll forget Julian Graves ever existed.'

'You're right,' Claudia said with a smile. 'I've been behaving like a spoiled child, and I'm sorry. Maybe I'll even call Jenny and see if I can talk her into changing her mind and taking me back on again.'

As the two women sat in the sunny kitchen, drinking coffee and munching on the fresh rolls, Claudia began to feel more like her old self. Laura was right. He wasn't worth it. From the meadow came the bleating protests of the sheep as her brother and the hired men sheared the first coats of the season. Soon Peter would be coming in for lunch.

'Laura,' she said. 'Please don't say anything to Peter about what's happened. You know, about Julian Graves and me.'

Laura raised horrified eyebrows heavenward. 'Heaven forbid!' she intoned piously. 'I wouldn't dream of it. Julian Graves is not his favourite person to begin with. He can't forgive him for cutting down those trees, even though I've argued myself blue in the face trying to convince him he only took out the ones that were old and rotten anyway. But try to tell Peter anything once he has his mind made up! And you know what he'd do if he found out the man had hurt his only sister.'

Claudia nodded grimly. 'I have a rough idea, and I think it would entail a shotgun.'

Both women started to laugh at the picture of grey-haired Peter marching over to Julian Graves' place with his gun cocked, ready to defend his sister's honour. Suddenly famished, after days of near-starvation, Claudia reached for another sticky roll.

It would be all right. Here she was, loved, protected, cherished. In time, she *would* forget Julian Graves ever existed.

CHAPTER FIVE

'How's the garden coming?' Peter asked that night at dinner. 'I haven't seen you up there for weeks.'

Claudia and Laura exchanged a quick, conspiratorial glance, united in their determination to keep Peter blissfully ignorant of what had happened between Claudia and Julian Graves.

'Oh, it hasn't been that long,' Claudia managed to say casually at last. 'Besides, the weather hasn't been very inspiring.'

'No,' Laura agreed hastily. 'It's been so—so——'

Peter raised a quizzical eyebrow and stared at his wife. 'So—what?' he asked mildly. 'We've had nothing but sunshine for several days.' He shovelled in another mouthful of lasagne, chewed, swallowed, and grunted contentedly. 'Good meal, Laura. As always.' He smiled benignly at his wife, then turned to Claudia with a sterner expression. 'In case you didn't know it, little sister, a garden isn't like a piece of furniture or a rock. It needs constant care, constant attention.'

'That's right,' she agreed quickly and gave him an overbright smile. 'You're absolutely right, Peter. Isn't he, Laura?'

'Oh, yes. Absolutely.'

Peter gazed suspiciously from one to the other. Both women were now busily engaged in finishing their dinner, and neither would meet his eyes. With a frown, he put his hands on the arms of his chair and pushed it back with a loud scraping sound.

'What the hell's going on here?' he asked in a baffled tone.

'Nothing,' they replied in unison.

Sighing with resignation, he got up from his chair, stretched widely and headed for the door. 'OK,' he called over his shoulder. 'Go ahead and keep your girlish secrets. I've got a sick ewe to look after.'

When he was gone and they heard the front door slam loudly behind him, they took one look at each other and started to giggle. Before long they were both bent over double, choking with laughter, the tears streaming down their cheeks.

Finally, Laura wiped her eyes and got up to clear the table. 'I'd better get this mess cleaned up before he comes back for his coffee,' she said, still chuckling and shaking her head. 'Or he *will* get suspicious.'

'Poor Peter,' Claudia said as she followed Laura into the kitchen with a stack of dirty plates.

Laura turned on the tap at the sink and started to rinse the glasses and silverware. 'Oh, Peter will survive,' she said airily, with a toss of her head.

'Well, thanks for not telling him about Julian.' She handed Laura the dishes.

Laura rolled her eyes. 'I wouldn't dream of it. I learned years ago what it was safe to confide to your brother and what would lead to an explosion.' She began to stack cutlery and china in the dishwasher. 'He's a wonderful man and an ideal husband, but he does have a temper.'

'How well I know,' Claudia commented drily.

They worked silently and efficiently, side by side, and when the kitchen was tidied up at last Laura wiped her hands on a towel and hung it neatly over the rack beneath the counter. Before switching off the overhead light, she gave Claudia a tentative look.

'He's right, you know,' she said quietly. 'You really should pay more attention to the garden. It's not only good exercise, but marvellous mental therapy. There's something about digging in the dirt, a sort of monotonous rhythm, that I find very soothing. Why don't you give it another try?'

'Oh, Laura, I couldn't! What if . . .'

Laura smiled wryly. 'What if you ran into Julian up there?' She shrugged and spread her hands wide. 'Well, so what if you did? It's your property. You have a perfect right to be there. Why should you let him keep you away?'

Claudia bit her lip and stared down at her leg. It had been such a warm day that she'd put on a pair of shorts late that afternoon for the first time since she had come back to Hidden Harbour. The angry red scars that had stretched from her upper thigh down over her knee across her calf, clear to her ankle, had faded by now into a dull, pinkish colour.

'It's still a good-looking leg,' Laura said softly. 'And when that scar fades a little more, it'll be a leg any woman would be proud of.'

Claudia gingerly flexed the wasted calf muscle, and winced at the shaft of pain that shot through her. It was worse than it had been, and she knew why. She'd been a fool to neglect her exercises, to refuse to co-operate with patient Jenny in the therapy sessions.

She looked at Laura. 'It's not going to be easy,' she said with a sigh.

'No,' Laura agreed promptly. 'Nothing worth while ever is. You, of all people, should know that. Look at what you had to go through to become a successful dancer, the iron determination it took to keep at it when you were ready to drop with exhaustion, when you had to fight through those discouraging failures along the way.'

'That's different,' Claudia protested. 'Dancing is a gift, a talent I was born with. I didn't earn it.'

'Oh, Claudia! We're all born with certain gifts, but it takes hard work and determination to use them properly.

Claudia glanced down at the leg again. Perhaps Laura was right. Maybe her legs would never dance again, but she didn't need to be ashamed to show them. Maybe with a tan . . .

'You're right,' she said. Then, more firmly, 'You're *absolutely* right! In fact, I'm going to call Jenny right now and *beg* her to come back to me.' She took Laura's hand and gave it a quick squeeze. 'Thanks, pal,' she said.

The next morning, fired with conviction after her first good night's sleep in a long time, Claudia set out after breakfast for her little garden plot, trowel and bucket in hand, ready to tackle the chore of making up for her neglect.

It was a beautiful day, calm and clear, with a hot sun already beating down. The deep blue water of the channel sparkled, the gulls were screeching on the rocks down by the shore and, in the distance, the pleasure boat bringing tourists over from the mainland was just chugging into the tiny harbour.

Still buoyed up and carried along by her renewed sense of determination, she'd worn her skimpiest pair of old exercise shorts and a brief halter-top. As she walked along, it even seemed to her that her limp was much improved, in spite of her recent spell of inactivity.

Half-way there, she stopped to rest. As she looked

around at the green fields, the sheep contentedly chomping on the fresh grass, a baby rabbit hopping along after its mother towards a nearby thicket of brush, her eye fell on the figure of a man directly in her line of vision. At this distance, she couldn't tell which side of the stone fence he was working, but a cold chill gripped her at the possibility that it might be Julian.

Her heart simply stopped beating for several seconds, then began to pound in heavy, sickening thuds. The goose-flesh stood out on her bare arms, and she had to grit her teeth to keep from turning tail and running back to the safety of the house. What would he do if he saw her? Ignore her? Turn away in disgust? Or would she see pity in the grey eyes? She didn't think she could bear his pity.

But Julian Graves was not a compassionate man, she reminded herself. He was cold, cruel, brutal and heartless. A genuine, dyed-in-the-wool bastard, in fact.

This unflattering assessment of the man's character made her feel much better. The hell with him, she thought. She wasn't going to let him keep her off her own property! She squared her shoulders and continued on, her head held high and without the slightest attempt to disguise her limp.

As she gradually came nearer the bent figure, she saw that it wasn't Julian after all, but Floyd Hopper, one of the hired men, out repairing the fence. When the man riased his head and waved at her, she could have kissed him. If it hadn't been the balding, chunky, tobacco-chewing Floyd, she might have done just that. Instead, she waved back gaily, called out a cheerful good morning, and kept on.

When she reached the fenced-in area that *used* to

be her garden, she stood there, staring inside, appalled at the havoc wrought by a mere two weeks of neglect. The hyacinth blossoms were shivelled and drooping on their thick, fleshy stalks, the primroses were buried under a jungle of weeds, and bright yellow dandelions bloomed profusely over what seemed like every square inch of the small plot of ground.

With a deep sigh, she lowered herself awkwardly to her knees, took up her trowel, and grimly set to work.

'Now, that's more like it,' Jenny said with satisfaction after that morning's therapy session.

When Claudia had called her three nights ago, she'd agreed readily to come back for their usual session on Friday, and she stood beside the exercise table now, beaming down at Claudia with an almost maternal pride shining out of her brown eyes.

'You think there's still hope, then?' Claudia groaned. She raised herself up carefully. It seemed that every muscle in her body was sore, both from the session with Jenny and yesterday's work in the garden.

'Of course I do, you ninny!' Jenny exclaimed with a snort. 'What have I been telling you all these months?' She gave Claudia a long, close look. 'You look as though you've been getting some sun, too. Your colour has even improved.'

Claudia slid off the table and slipped her robe on. 'Yes. I had a long session in the garden yesterday. I decided my poor posies needed attention far more than my own depressing thoughts.'

Jenny laughed and put an arm around her shoulders. 'Good for you.'

'Do you have time for coffee?' Claudia asked as they walked down the hall. 'I think Laura's been baking again.'

'Sorry, I have to run.' She sniffed the air. 'Although I'm tempted. It beats me why the three of you aren't as fat as pigs. I've always envied you your figure, Claudia,' she said, with a rueful glance down at her own stocky frame. 'But I finally came to the conclusion it's in the bones.'

Claudia smiled. 'I don't know about that. And don't speak too soon. Laura seems bound and determined to fatten me up.'

'It won't hurt you to put on a few more pounds. You're still too thin.'

When Jenny left, Claudia stood at the open door, looking after her as the Toyota disappeared around the bend, and debating what to do with the rest of the morning. She could either sit in the kitchen with Laura and stuff herself, or she could go back to the garden.

Finally she made up her mind. 'Laura,' she called. 'I'll be out in the field until lunch. OK?'

'OK,' came the cheerful reply. 'Don't work too hard.'

It was another fine day, and Claudia had already learned that serious gardeners had to strike while the iron was hot to get the work done before another spell of rain set in. There would be plenty of wet days when she'd have to stay indoors.

Yesterday's labours hadn't made much of a dent in the rampant growth of weeds, but it did look a little less daunting to her today, enough at least to spur her on to keep at it.

She'd been working steadily in absorbed concentration for about an hour when suddenly she heard a noise coming from the other side of the stone fence, a rustling sound in the high grass, as though someone were walking towards her. Her heart caught in her throat. If it was Julian, she'd just have to face it. Slowly, she raised her eyes.

There, twenty feet away, sitting on top of the wall, was a small girl. She was dressed neatly in a pair of red shorts and a checked shirt, her sandalled feet dangling over the wall. Her long fair hair was tied in a ponytail, and she was gazing solemnly down at Claudia out of a pair of grey eyes that were startlingly familiar. Julian's daughter, she thought. What was her name? Margaret, that was it.

That's all I need, she thought. She looked away quickly and stabbed her trowel viciously at a clump of chickweek. Of course, it was not the girl's fault that her father was such a rotten person, but just the sight of those clear grey eyes was a painful reminder of the man's treachery. It had been an act of sheer cowardice that she would never forgive, and she was *not* going to get involved with that family again under any circumstances whatsoever.

She worked for another hour, studiously ignoring the silent child. By now the perspiration was streaming down her face under the hot sun, and her leg ached from stooping for so long. It was almost time for lunch, anyway, and she was more than ready to quit.

She had just dug out her last dandelion and set it on the pile of weeds when a loud clatter broke into the stillness, startling her. She looked and saw that the child was now standing on her own side of the wall. A loose stone must have fallen as she'd clambered down. She'd been so quiet that Claudia had forgotten she was even there, and she turned now, streaking across the neighbouring field towards home.

Still watching the small, retreating figure, Claudia raised herself up from the ground, stretched her aching muscles and wiped her filthy hands on the seat of her shorts. Then, just at the edge of the hill, before it sloped steeply downwards to the house, she saw the girl turn back.

They were more than a hundred feet apart by now, but even at that distance it seemed to Claudia that their eyes caught and held in a swift, silent form of communication. In fact, in the next moment, the child raised her hand, as though saluting her, and for a brief moment she was tempted to return the gesture. But she stayed motionless where she stood. There was no point in encouraging her.

The the girl turned around and continued on down the hill until she disappeared from view.

After one last, satisfied survey of her morning's work, Claudia picked up her tools and headed slowly back to the house. The child had made a profound impression on her, not only by her solemn silent appraisal, but by her obvious loneliness. It wasn't natural for an eight-year-old to spend a sunny summer morning sitting on a fence watching someone else garden.

Or was it? In a sudden flood of memory, she recalled that she had been just such a solitary child herself, and had sat on that same stone wall many a lazy morning, the insects buzzing around her, the smell of new-mown hay sweet on the hot summer air, watching her father or Peter or one of the hired men working in the fields, shearing the sheep, and dreaming about becoming a famous dancer.

Well, those dreams were over. For her own peace

of mind she had to harden herself against the little girl. She wanted nothing to do with her or her father. Even though Laura had convinced her she had nothing to be ashamed of, that the man was beneath contempt for the way he had treated her, she still shuddered with humiliation every time she thought of her mindless response to his skilful lovemaking.

When she reached the house, she noticed that the battered old station wagon belonging to Mrs Jacobs was parked in the drive. It was her day to come and help Laura clean. That meant a quick lunch at the kitchen counter, since Peter adamantly refused to put in even a token appearance for the meal when the voluble Mrs Jacobs was present, and Laura insisted on feeding her.

As Claudia went inside, she could already hear the high-pitched twang issuing from the kitchen. Maybe she could sneak upstairs and have her much-needed shower now, then grab a quick bite when Laura and Mrs Jacobs were back at work.

She limped as quietly as possible across the hall towards the stairs, and had her hand on the banister when she heard Laura call her name.

'Claudia?'

She turned around guiltily to face a pair of accusing pale blue eyes. 'Yes, Laura,' she said with a sigh. 'What is it?'

'Aren't you going to join us for lunch?'

'I need a shower badly, Laura,' she protested, but without much conviction. She held out her grimy hands. 'I'm filthy.' But she knew it would be no use. Mild-mannered Laura could be quite firm once her mind was made up to something.

'I have your milk poured and your sandwich all made. You don't want it to dry out.'

'No. All right. Let me just wash up first.'

'You can do that in the kitchen.'

Since Laura obviously had no intention of letting her out of her sight, there went her one chance of escape. She turned back and followed her into the kitchen, where Mrs Jacobs, a short, skinny woman with a gaunt, hawklike face and piercing black eyes, was sitting at the counter, tucking into the enormous lunch Laura always fixed for her on "her day".

'Well, Miss Claudia!' she shrieked. 'Aren't you looking chipper this morning! Been out working in your little garden?'

'Yes, I have.' Claudia hoisted herself awkwardly up on the stool next to her, under the woman's voracious scrutiny.

'My, you get more use out of that leg every day, don't you, dear?' She leaned over and peered at the long scar in a thorough, searching and totally unabashed examination.

Claudia gritted her teeth and forced out a smile. 'How have you been, Mrs Jacobs?'

'Oh, I can't complain,' she replied, then proceeded to catalogue an interminable list of ailments and complaints about her "clients", ending up with, 'Of course, there's no pleasing Mr Graves, no matter what I do. I've given up trying.'

Claudia suppressed a smile as she recalled Julian's tale of how he had forbidden Mrs Jacobs to speak in his presence. 'And how is Mr Jacobs?' she asked, in an effort to steer the conversation away from that distasteful subject.

Mrs Jacobs dismissed her husband with an offhand, 'Oh, he's all right,' and proceeded to impart the latest titbit of gossip from the house next door. 'You know,' she said, lowering her voice to a confidential squawk, 'that man is no fit father for that poor little girl. Such carryings-on you wouldn't believe!' She rolled her eyes and nodded.

'Laura, would you please pass me the mustard?' Claudia, who detested mustard, said in desperation.

Laura idly shoved the jar of mustard in Claudia's direction, her eyes fixed all the while on the egregious Mrs Jacobs. 'What do you mean, carryings-on?' she asked, clearly entranced.

'Oh, you know. Locking himself up in that studio of his, shutting out that poor child, going off by himself, bringing that blonde hussy into the house.'

'Blonde hussy?' Laura prompted.

Mrs Jacobs nodded grimly. 'You know, that Sharon person from California. Says she's his agent, or some such nonsense. if you ask me, she's wanting to be the second Mrs Graves a sight more than she wants to sell his pictures.'

Claudia squirmed under this spate of unwanted information, but there was no stopping Laura, who was listening with rapt attention. 'Did you know the first Mrs Graves, then?' she asked, all innocence.

'Oh, my, yes! A lovely lady. Beautiful, too, and knew how to treat her help. Not like *him*.' She lowered her voice a decibel, so that it became a mere hoarse shout. 'He killed her, you know.'

Claudia's mouth dropped open and she set her half eaten sandwich down on its plate. 'He killed his wife?' she breathed.

Mrs Jacobs beamed with intense satisfaction at the reaction she'd finally elicited and nodded triumphantly. 'As good as. At least,' she amended in an offhanded tone of regret, 'he was driving the car the night they had the wreck that killed her.'

'That's not quite the same thing,' Laura pointed

out severely.

'Maybe so, but you can't tell me he wasn't glad when she was gone. Used to fight like cats and dogs, they did. She hated those pictures of his, said he stole the time from her, that he cared more about his so-called art than he did about her. But would he give them up to make her happy?' she enquired with a dramatic flourish. 'Not on your life!'

'But the man is an artist!' Claudia cried. 'He makes his living painting. You can't blame him for that. And to say he killed her is simply ridiculous.' She stopped short. What was she doing, defending the man who had behaved so badly to her, the man she thought of as her worst enemy? Even more to the point, what would Mrs Jacobs make of her outburst? Whatever it was, she could be sure it would be spread over the entire village by sundown. She could have bitten her tongue out.

Mrs Jacobs only sniffed, but she did back down a bit. 'That's all well and good, Miss Claudia,' she said airly, 'and certainly none of my concern. What worries me is Margaret, the little girl. Not that I object to looking after her when he's away, mind you. She's no trouble. A quiet little thing.' She shook her head. 'Not a normal child at all, though. Just mopes around, daydreaming. Poor little mite. That man is as cold as ice, can't even give his own motherless daughter a by-your-leave or time of day. Much less my insignificant self,' she added with another sniff. 'Treats me like a servant, he does.'

By then, Claudia had choked down her sandwich, gulped most of her milk, and was sliding off the stool, ready to make her getaway. She'd had enough—far more than enough—of gossip for one day.

She turned to Laura. 'Thanks for the lunch. Got to get under that shower, now. Right away,' she added firmly, to forestall any objections. 'Goodbye Mrs Jacobs. I'm glad to see you in such fine form.'

As she made her exit, she could hear the strident voice raised in a question. 'Fine form? Now what did she mean by that?' And she had no doubt that the innocuous statement would be inflated into far more interesting proportions for the delectation of all the odious woman's other clients on the island.

That night at dinner, Laura recounted Mrs Jacobs' latest news bulletin to Peter, who sat listening glumly throughout the entire recital. When she was through, he glowered balefully at her.

'That woman is a menace,' he said flatly. 'I don't know why you let her in the house.'

'But is what she said true? Do you think he was responsible for his wife's death?'

'How should I know? Besides, even if he was, that doesn't make him a murderer.'

'I thought you didn't like him,' his wife said mildly.

'I don't even know the man!' Peter exploded. 'I just don't like him cutting down those trees, that's all.'

With that, he fixed his eyes firmly on his plate, a sure sign that the conversation was over as far as he was concerned, and Laura turned to Claudia.

'It's a pity about the little girl, though. No mother. A father who neglects her. Have you seen any sign of her when you've been up in the meadow working?'

'Just a glimpse,' Claudia replied shortly. She turned to her brother. 'By the way, Peter, did you remember to pick up the bedding plants for me at the nursery today?'

'Yes. They're still in the back of the truck. Are you ready to plant them?'

'I will be soon. I should have it cleared of weeds in a day or two.'

'Want help carrying them up there?'

'No, thanks. I can manage. What did you get me?'

With the topic of conversation now safely on a neutral subject, they finished dinner in a heated discussion of the relative merits of perennials and annuals.

At the end of the next week, it was actually beginning to look like a real garden. The weeds were gone entirely, and clumps of brightly coloured blooming plants rose up in their place.

Although she worked facing away from the stone wall, Claudia was acutely conscious that Margaret Graves was somewhere on the other side, just as she had been every other day. They still hadn't spoken a word to each other, and, although she still had an occasional twinge of guilt about the way she ignored the girl so pointedly, after the awkwardness of that first day she gradually began to feel more at ease in her silent, watchful presence.

Sometimes Margaret would sit quite still for an hour at a time, while at others she would suddenly start running like a little wild thing through the grass towards the pond, twirling and skipping in what looked like an awkward attempt at dance steps.

This skirting so close to the water made Claudia nervous at first, and aroused a new wave of resentment against a man who allowed his daughter to court danger in such a fashion. She soon realised however, that with an uncanny sense of self-preservation the girl always did stop right at the edge, and, since the pond was really quite shallow for several feet, there was no real danger.

Still, it annoyed her to be put in the position of unpaid baby-sitter, and it took all her will-power to keep her eyes firmly averted from the girl's antics and concentrate on her work.'

When she'd patted earth around the last geranium, she stood up and surveyed her handiwork with satisfaction. It really was coming along quite nicely. Now that the summer sun seemed to be here to stay, she'd have to ask Peter about getting water to it next.

Suddenly, from the distance, she heard a man's voice calling, 'Margaret, Margaret! Where are you?'

As the voice came closer, Claudia knew it had to be Julian, come to look for his daughter at last, and she froze where she stood. Since that last awful night in front of the house, she hadn't set eyes on him once. She took in a deep breath and fought down the impulse to turn and run away before he got any nearer.

Then, out of the corner of her eye, she saw Margaret come running up from the pond. 'Daddy, Daddy,' she called. 'Here I am!' She raced towards her approaching father and flung herself at him.

He gripped the child roughly by her thin shoulders and held her at a distance. 'Margaret, he said in a voice shaking with emotion. 'How many times have I told you never to come up here alone?'

The beast, Claudia thought, and almost trod on a pink petunia. Has he no heart at all? Although she only managed a brief surreptitious glance at the painful scene, her heart ached for the little girl. She recalled her own father coming up to the meadow many times looking for her when she was a child. She would run to him, throwing herself at him in the same way, and would never forget how he would pick her up, laughing, and hold her high in his strong arms.

'But, Daddy,' the girl said, 'Mrs Jacobs said I could. And I'm not alone. *She's* here.'

To her horror, Claudia saw Margaret turn and point directly at her. There was no escape now. In his anger with the girl, Julian obviously hadn't noticed her before. That's when she should have left. Now it was too late. He'd seen her, and he was gazing directly into her eyes. She made herself stand perfectly still.

Then, to her utter surprise, his glance faltered. He looked uncertainly down at his daughter, and for a moment Claudia expected he would simply turn around and leave. Instead, he took Margaret by the hand and began to walk slowly towards the wall. He stared over it at her colourful garden for a few seconds, then raised his eyes to meet hers.

'Hello, Claudia,' he said in a low voice.

It gradually dawned on Claudia that she was the one in command of the situation, a situation she had dreaded for weeks. He was at a distinct disadvantage, and it was clear he knew it as well as she did. Thrilled beyond measure at his obvious embarrassment, Claudia gave him a cool smile.

'Hello, Julian,' she replied in an even tone. 'Lovely day.' With a brief nod, she bent down to collect her trowel, then turned and started walking away.

She hadn't gone five feet when she heard him call her name. She stopped, hesitated, then decided that, since she held the cards, she might as well play out her hand to the end and extract the maximum satisfaction from it. She turned around.

'Yes. What is it?'

He lifted Margaret up and set her on top of the wall. 'Stay there for a minute,' he said. Then, in a swift, graceful movement, he vaulted over it on to the other side and walked slowly towards her, his hands shoved in the pockets of his dark trousers, his shoulders hunched forward, and a dark scowl on his lean, tanned face.

As Claudia watched him approach, she once again had to admire the man's good looks and graceful, athletic stride, but she was also pleased to note that she could do so quite dispassionately now, without a hint of desire. She had no idea what he wanted to say to her, but she hoped fervently that whatever it was it would give her an opportunity to twist the knife a little harder.

He was standing before her now, so close that when he raised his bent head to look at her again she could see the dark flecks in his grey eyes, the little lines at the corners. He ran a hand through his thick, dark hair, which once again badly needed cutting, and frowned down at the ground, as though searching for the proper words.

'I've been meaning to speak to you,' he said at last.

'Oh? What about?'

A dark red flush passed over his face at that. 'About why I didn't come to you as I said I would,' he said roughly.

'Oh, that,' she said, with a little offhand laugh. 'Don't give it another thought. I quite understand. It happens sometimes. It doesn't matter in the slightest.'

'Perhaps not,' he said stiffly. 'Still, I feel I owe you an explanation.' He raised a hand tentatively, as though to reach out and touch her, and she drew back, her face hardening.

'Forget it, Julian. You owe me absolutely nothing. Now, I've really got to go. My family is expecting me.'

With one last curt nod of dismissal, she turned and walked away from him, her head held high. Even though she could feel his eyes burning into her every step of the way, she made no attempt to disguise her limp, and once she was safely out of earshot, she began to mutter under her breath, 'I've done it. I've won. I've really won!'

CHAPTER SIX

THE next day when Claudia went up to the meadow and saw Margaret sitting on her perch, she assumed that either she had obtained her father's permission to venture this far from the house, or he was safely out of town again and she was left under Mrs Jacobs' careless jurisdiction.

After the way Julian had treated the girl yesterday, Claudia's reservations about getting involved were forgotten, and today she gave the girl a friendly smile. Immediately, she beamed back at her.

'My name is Margaret,' she said.

'Yes, I know. And mine is Claudia.'

Claudia bent down with her trowel to cultivate the earth around her new plants, and for the next half-hour neither of them spoke again. Margaret murmured or hummed softly to herself in broken snatches of a nursery tune from time to time, and it wasn't an uncomfortable silence.

Finally, when Claudia sat back to rest, the girl apparently saw it as a signal that it was all right to speak again.

'My dadddy said you're a dancer.'

'That's right. Rather,' she amended, 'I *was* a dancer.'

Margaret nodded solemnly. 'Then you hurt your leg.'

'Yes,' Claudia replied softly. 'Then I hurt my leg.'

'I'm very sorry.'

'Thank you, Margaret. I'm sorry, too.'

There was another short silence. Claudia leaned back against the trunk of the tree and closed her eyes. After a few minutes, the girl said, 'Does it hurt?'

Claudia looked at her and smiled. 'My leg? Not so much any more.'

'That's good.' She paused, then said shyly. 'I want to be a dancer, too.'

Claudia examined the small body with a critical eye. It was hard to tell, but it looked at though Margaret might have the good bones and slender frame a dancer needed.

'It takes a lot of hard work to become a good dancer,' she said. 'You have to want it more than anything else.'

'Oh, I do!'

'Don't you have anyone to play with up here?' Claudia asked. 'There are lots of children in the village.'

'I live with my aunt in California when I go to school,' the girl replied. 'So I don't know anyone here. Besides, I don't like games much. I'd rather learn to dance.'

Warning herself to tread cautiously on such slippery ground, Claudia asked, 'Have you told your father that?'

'Yes, but he's very busy. He's a famous painter, you know,' she added with obvious pride. 'He doesn't have much time for me.'

The brute, Claudia thought. Then inspiration hit her. She knew she shouldn't interfere, but she couldn't help feeling sorry for the girl. 'I think there are summer classes at the community centre in the village,' she said carefully. 'They used to give dancing lessons. Perhaps they still do. Maybe if you asked your father about it, he'd look into it for you.'

Margaret brightened at that. 'I could ask, couldn't I?' Then her face fell. 'But he's gone again. He and Sharon went off to California together.'

'I see,' Claudia said in a tight voice.

'I don't suppose you could do it for me?' Margaret asked shyly. 'I mean, find out about the lessons.'

Do *not* get involved, Claudia warned herself again sternly. She looked at Margaret's eager face and felt her resolve weakening. On the other hand, what harm would it do to enquire? The community centre used to put out brochures advertising their summer schedule for the benefit of the tourists. She could at least see if they were still available the next time she went into the village.

'I'll see what I can do,' she said at last.

'Do you reaise,' Laura said one morning some weeks later, 'that it's almost the end of July?'

'Hard to believe,' Claudia replied idly. She was just finishing a last cup of coffee after breakfast, and another long day loomed ahead of her.

Laura sighed heavily. 'Every year seems to go by faster after forty.'

Claudia murmured an indistinct reply. She found herself becoming more and more restless every day. The tourist season was in full swing, and the yearly influx of boaters crowded the harbour. The streets of the village literally teemed with them, causing much grumbling among the natives, who were all beginning to long for the autumn, when they would have the island to themselves again.

'What are you going to do today?' Laura asked.

'Oh, I don't know. Maybe talk a walk up to the garden.'

'How's it coming?'

Claudia smiled. 'It doesn't really need me any more, except for a little weeding and an occasional watering.'

Laura gave her a long, silent look, then said, 'Have you heard anything from Charles lately?'

'No. You know I haven't.'

'I thought maybe you might be reconsidering his teaching offer. Or,' she added with a smile, 'any other offer he happened to have made when he was here in May.'

'Oh, not really.' She stifled a yawn and got up from the table. 'I don't know what I want to do. Right now, I guess I'll go take my walk.'

As she dawdled her way slowly up to the meadow, it occurred to her suddenly how much she missed Margaret's company. True to her word, she had indeed found that the village centre still offered dancing classes. She had presented the brochure to Margaret, and apparently the girl had either received permission from her father to attend, or else Mrs Jacobs had taken it upon herself to enrol her. In any case, she hadn't been back to the meadow since then.

Now, as Claudia approached the garden, she was surprised—and glad—to see the girl sitting on the wall, obviously waiting for her. When she saw Claudia, she smiled and waved.

'Where have you been?' Claudia called. 'I've missed you.'

'I've been taking dancing lessons,' Margaret announced proudly.

'Well, they must be agreeing with you,' Claudia said with a grin. She had reached the wall now, and the change in the girl was astounding. Her grey eyes sparkled, her cheeks were suffused with colour, and the dull, listless look was gone.

'Would you like to see the steps I've learned so far?'

'Why, yes, I'd love to.'

'I'll have to come over to your side so you can see me,' she said hesitantly. 'Is that all right?'

'Of course. Can you manage all right on your own?'

'Oh, sure.'

She scrambled to her knees, raised herself up, and stood balanced precariously on top of the wall. She was just getting ready to jump down on Claudia's side, when all of a sudden her foot jarred a large stone loose, and it came clattering down. Claudia gave a little cry and rushed forward but, before she could reach her, Margaret had already lost her footing and fallen in a heap on the ground, where she now lay, shrieking with pain.

'Oh, ow, ow!' she sobbed.

By the time Claudia had knelt down beside her, the girl had struggled to a sitting position and was holding her ankle, still howling, and rocking back and forth.

Claudia put an arm around her and stroked her hair. 'Now, now,' she soothed. 'I know it hurts. Dancers do this to themselves all the time. You must try to be brave. Now, let me take a look at it to see what you've done.'

Margaret gave her a piteous look, sniffled loudly and wiped her tear-streaked face, obviously trying hard to stop crying. She nodded, and Claudia began to probe gently around the ankle, which was already beginning to swell. Very carefully, she tried moving it slightly to make sure it wasn't broken.

'Well, that's all right, then,' she said with an

encouraging smile. 'It's either a slight sprain or a pulled ligament. I'm afraid you'll probably have to miss your next few lessons, though.' When she saw the girl's stricken look, she added hastily, 'But you can still practise your hand positions. They're very important.'

She stood up then and gazed all around at the empty fields. She sighed with frustration. There wasn't another soul in sight in any direction. Margaret couldn't possibly manage to get home on her own without further damage to her ankle, and she couldn't just leave her out here alone.

There was no way out of it. She'd just have to help the girl home herself. She bent down and held Margaret under her shoulders, pulling her carefully up to her feet.

'Come on,' she said. 'Let's see if you can put any weight on that ankle. There, that's all right then.' She gave her an encouraging smile, and they set off.

Little by little, and hobbling all the way, they did manage to traverse the field that led down the hill. When they came in sight of Julian's house, Claudia stopped short, worn out from the extra weight of the girl leaning on her.

'We make quite a pair, don't we?' she said, panting.

Margaret looked up at her. 'What's wrong? Are you tired?'

'A little.' She thought for a minute. They were close enough now that Margaret might be able to make it to the house without her help. 'Margaret, is your father home?'

'Oh, no. He and Sharon had to go to California again for an important exhibition in San Francisco, and he won't be home until tomorrow.'

'How about Mrs Jacobs?'

'She always watches television or takes a nap in the afternoon.'

Claudia silently cursed Mrs Jacobs. There was nothing for it. She'd have to see to it herself. The ankle needed cold compresses, and should be looked at by a doctor.

The house was surrounded by large cherry trees which, Claudia observed drily to herself, somehow had escaped Julian's axe, and it was cool on the wide, paved terrace.

'Let's go in the back way,' Margaret said, opening a screen door. 'Then I can show you Daddy's studio on the way.'

'I don't think that's such a good idea,' Claudia said dubiously as she followed her down a wide, oak-floored hallway.

'Oh, Daddy doesn't care. Just so long as we don't touch anything. He's very particular about that.'

The first door they came to was slightly ajar. Margaret pushed it open all the way, and Claudia gaze out over her head at an astonishing array of dark, sombre paintings: seascapes, landscapes, still lifes, a few starkly elongated figures, all in the same dull blues and greys, with here and there a streak of black or white for emphasis.

She stared around, wide-eyed and speechless, deeply impressed by the power and emotion the paintings managed to convey, in spite of their muted colours, but at the same time appalled by the deep melancholy that pervaded each one.

Margaret was tugging at her hand. 'Come on,' she said. 'I want to show you something.'

She led her over to the far wall, where several canvases were stacked against it, wrong side facing towards them. Releasing Claudia's hand, she leaned over and turned the top one around, then looked up at her with a wide grin of anticipation.

'Well?' she said. 'What do you think of that?'

Claudia could only stare, stunned by what she saw. It was so different from the others as to be painted by another hand altogether. But that wasn't all. There on the canvas was a half-finished, full-length figure of a dancer, and if she had sat for it herself it couldn't have been more like her.

The figure was posed in a graceful position, facing sideways and slightly bent over, the hands poised over her head, one foot pointing forward, the other to the side. It was her smooth, dark hair, pulled back in a tight bun at the top of her head, her face, her body—and without a stitch of clothing on it.

Claudia's mouth fell open, and her face went up in flame. How dared he do such a thing? After a moment she felt Margaret tugging at her hand, and she glanced down at her. Her face was screwed into a worried expression.

'Does it embarrass you, Claudia? Daddy says the human body is a beautiful work of art. So it can't be wrong, can it?'

'No, no, of course not,' Claudia assured her hurriedly. All she wanted to do was get out of there. 'And thank you very much for showing it to me. But now I think we'd better get that ankle taken care of.'

She waited impatiently while Margaret carefully turned the canvas to the wall again, then made for the door, hurrying the girl along so fast that she didn't see the loose tile until suddenly Margaret's toe came up against it, and she stumbled. Horrified at her carelessness, Claudia caught at her, but it was too late. With a loud cry, the girl went sprawling, coming down right on her injured ankle, and immediately started crying.

Claudia bent down beside her, but before she could even take in what had happened she heard footsteps come running down the hall towards them. Then a pair of long, dark-trousered legs appeared, and she looked up to see Julian Graves standing before her, his face drawn and haggard.

'What happened?' he said in a tight voice. He knelt down on the floor and gathered the sobbing child awkwardly into his arms. 'What is it, Margaret?'

'She had a fall,' Claudia said shakily. 'I don't think it's serious.'

He glared at her. 'It's that damned dancing,' he ground out.

'It has nothing whatsoever to do with dancing,' Claudia replied heatedly.

She was about to tell him in no uncertain terms that, if he'd stay home and pay more attention to his only child instead of gallivanting around California with gorgeous blondes, maybe these things wouldn't happen, when she recognised the look in his haunted grey eyes. It was fear. Stark, staring fear.

'It's all right,' she said in a gentler tone. 'There's no real harm done. Children fall all the time.'

'What should I do?' he choked out.'

Margaret's screams had subsided by now, and she was sobbing quietly into her father's shoulder, her arms twined around his neck. Julian's face was drained of all colour, and he held on to the girl as though afraid she would disintegrate if he loosened his grip on her.

Claudia rose to her feet. 'Come on,' she said briskly. 'I think we should soak the foot in cold water first to take down the swelling, then put her to bed and call the doctor. Where's the bathroom?'

'Right down the hall,' he replied meekly.

He scooped the girl up in his arms and led the way to a large tiled bath, carrying Margaret like a fragile piece of porcelain. Claudia ran cold water in the tub, and while the ankle was soaking Julian called the local doctor, who confirmed that cold water, aspirin and bed rest were the proper treatment until he had time to come out to examine her later that afternoon.

They finally got Margaret safely tucked up in bed, the ankle raised on a pillow. With the help of a children's dose of aspirin, and worn out from the trauma and excitement of her injury, she was asleep five minutes after her head hit the pillow.

With Margaret taken care of and the chastened Mrs Jacobs ensconced in a chair by the side of the sleeping child's bed, it was time for Claudia to leave. Now that the emergency was over and Margaret taken care of, she was uncomfortable in Julian's house, and she, too, was tired out from her morning's exertions.

'She'll be all right now,' she said as they walked down the hall. 'Mrs Jacobs feels so guilty at her neglect that I think you can count on her to stick with it this time. It's time I was getting home.'

'I'll drive you,' Julian said.

She was about to protest, but common sense told her that she was in no shape to make that long trip on foot across both Julian's field and her own. She gave him a dubious look.

'Please,' he said quietly. 'It's the least I can do. If you hadn't been there to help her when she fell, she could still be lying up there, injured and helpless.' His face grew thunderous. 'That damned Mrs Jacobs!' he muttered darkly.

'Oh, don't be too hard on Mrs Jacobs. No one can

watch an active child one hundred per cent of the time. Accidents do happen, you know. You can't protect children perfectly.'

He gave her a grim look. 'Perhaps not, but one can try.'

And where have you been all summer when your child needed you? was her unspoken thought. Either he could read her mind, or her expression gave her away, because he stiffened immediately and gave her a grim look.

'I was under the impression that Mrs Jacobs was fond of Margaret,' he said stiffly. 'She assured me constantly that she watched her like a hawk. At least, that's what I'm paying her an exorbitant salary to do. It's just damned lucky I came back a day early.'

'I'm sure Mrs Jacobs does her best,' she said, then added pointedly, 'but paid help can never replace a loving parent. Anyway, all's well that ends well, and I think now I'll take you up on that offer of a lift home.' She lifted her chin and gave him a direct look. 'My bad leg is rather aching.'

As he met her eyes, a dark red flush spread across his face. He started to say something, then apparently changed his mind. Instead he turned and started walking down the hall towards the front of the house. She followed him silently, wondering what it was he had been about to say to her.

At the door to the kitchen, he stopped short and turned back to her. 'Mrs Jacobs has already made lunch. Will you stay and eat with me?'

She hesitated, frowning. 'I don't know, Julian,' she said.

'Please. I'd like to talk to you.'

For a moment, she was tempted. What harm could it do? She was immune to his charms now. He could never hurt her again. She had become very fond of Margaret, and there was no point in prolonging hostilities with her father. She'd won her point, after all.

Then his voice softened and his eyes roamed over her appreciatively. 'You're looking very lovely. I've missed you.'

She didn't at all like the way he was eyeing her so speculatively, like a tender morsel just dished up on his plate. The last thing she wanted to do was encourage him or give him the idea that she was ready to fall into his arms the moment he crooked his little finger.

'I don't think so, Julian,' she said quietly. 'Laura will be expecting me for lunch.'

'You could call her.'

She shook her head. 'No. I can't stay.'

'You mean, you don't want to stay,' he stated flatly. She was all ready with a stinging retort when he raised a hand in the air. 'Don't say it. I don't blame you. I behaved abominably to you, I admit. But I would like a chance to explain.'

An insidious warmth began to spread through her as the memory of that humiliating episode came flooding back into her mind. The thought of the way she'd behaved that night, like a naïve, gullible fool, and all over a man with a chunk of ice for a heart, still had the power to wound and sicken her.

'I told you once before there was no need to explain anything to me, Julian, and if you don't mind, I'd really rather not discuss it. Not now. Not ever again.'

His face darkened at that. 'But, damn it, I *want* to discuss it. I *need* to discuss it.'

She squared her shoulders and looked him straight in the eye. 'And what makes what *you* want of such overwhelming importance?' she said in a low voice that throbbed with contempt. 'Believe me, Julian, what you want is the last thing in the world that interests me. Now, are you going to drive me home, or shall I call Peter to come and get me?'

For several moments they stood there in the hall, glaring at each other. Claudia was uncomfortably aware that her chest was heaving with emotion, her breath coming in painful, shuddering gusts, tightening the thin material of her halter-top over her breasts, and she had a sudden mental vision of that nude portrait of her in his studio.

She was determined not to back down an inch, however, and stood her ground firmly, her arms held rigid at her sides and her hands clutched into fists. Then, to her intense satisfaction, he gave her a twisted smile and narrowed his eyes at her.

'Spiteful, unforgiving little thing, aren't you?' he said lightly. 'Stubborn, too. Come on, then. I'll drive you home.'

He led the way out through the front door on to a wide, shady courtyard, and they walked together over the brick paving to where his dark, foreign car was parked in the shade of the house. He opened the door for her, and she got inside.

As she watched him walk around the front of the car in his quick, athletic stride, she felt a sharp pang of regret that things had worked out the way they had. He still had the power to attract her, and it took some fancy mental footwork to remind herself firmly that that was the best reason in the world why she had to stay away from him.

He got in beside her and fired the engine. 'I noticed your leg seems much better.' He spoke in a casual tone, and without looking at her. 'You hardly limp at all now.'

She stared straight ahead, unblinking. 'Yes,' she muttered. 'It is.'

Then he laid his arm on the back of her seat, twisted his head towards her, and skilfully backed the car around so that it faced the driveway. Claudia's cheeks burned, both from the hated reference to her limp and the close proximity of his lean, tanned face to hers.

He drove quite slowly over the narrow country road, and for some time neither of them spoke again. Finally, he glanced over at her and said, 'What I've been trying to explain to you is why I didn't come back when I said I would, why I've stayed away from you for so long.'

'Julian——' she began in a warning tone.

But this time he wouldn't be stopped. To her dismay, he pulled abruptly off the road on to a gravel shoulder, parked the car under a clump of trees and switched off the motor. Then, with his hands gripping the steering wheel, he began to speak in a low, flat voice.

'Whether you like it or not,' he ground out, 'you've got to hear me out. It's been driving me mad for weeks, and I simply won't let another day go by without at least telling you what really happened that night.'

She turned on him angrily. 'Look, Julian, I *know* why you walked out on me, and I admit it hurt at the time. But I'm over that now. I had a lot of adjustments to make after I found out I'd never dance again, never even walk straight again, for God's sake!' She took a deep breath and turned away. 'But I don't blame you any more. You're an artist, a seeker after perfection. I understand that, when you found out I would be a cripple for the rest of my life, you simply didn't want anything more to do with me.'

'It's not at all what you think. I know it looked like that, but believe me, it wasn't.'

Claudia lapsed into a sullen silence and mentally closed her eyes and her heart against him. She didn't want to hear what he had to say, and she bitterly regretted not calling Peter to come for her. Even walking back across those hot fields would be better than this.

'Please take me home, now,' she said, turning away from him and gazing stonily out the window.

'God, you're stubborn,' he said in an exasperated tone. 'What do I have to do to make you listen to me? Damn it, I *like* you, I'm very attracted to you. Won't you at least give me a chance to explain?'

'No,' she replied dully. 'I just want to go home.'

With a muttered curse, he reached down, twisted the key in the ignition viciously, and with a loud spurt of gravel sped back on to the road. They drove the rest of the distance to her house in a miserable silence, the warm air inside the car virtually crackling with heavy, electrically charged tension.

When they finally pulled off the road and started down the drive that wound down to the front of the house, Claudia noticed a strange car in the driveway. Peter and Laura were standing out on the porch talking to a man. His back was towards her but, as they came closer, Claudia immediately recognised Charles Thornton's fair head and stocky form.

The one thing she didn't want was for the two men to meet. When they came within twenty feet of the house, within easy walking distance, Claudia turned to Julian and said, 'Let me out here, please. I can walk the rest of the way.'

He didn't even answer her. He just kept on grimly driving straight ahead as though she'd never spoken, until he pulled up right behind the other car. The minute he stepped on the brake, she flung open the door and got outside.

'Thank you for the lift,' she gritted through her teeth, then slammed the door hard and started walking towards the others without a backward glance.

Although she could still hear the motor idling, there wasn't a sign that he had any intention of leaving, nor any sound of the car turning around. 'Why doesn't he just leave?' she muttered under her breath as she limped along.

Charles had turned around at the sound of Julian's car, and when he saw Claudia his face immediately broke into a broad smile of welcome and he hurried towards her, his arms outstretched.

'Oh, Charles,' she breathed. 'It's so good to see you.'

He kissed her lightly on the mouth, then held her from him and gazed down at her, his kind hazel eyes alight with affection. 'You look marvellous, Claudia,' he said. 'Absolutely blooming.' He glanced down at her leg. 'And that's not even noticeable. I'm so proud of you.'

With his arm still around her shoulder, he turned, and they started walking slowly towards Peter and Laura. At the same time, Claudia heard Julian's car turn and roar off up the driveway. Thank God, she thought. She glanced at her brother, who was frowning at the retreating vehicle.

'Who was that?' he asked suspiciously.

'Oh, just Julian Graves,' she said in an offhand tone.

'What the hell does he want?'

'He just gave me a ride home, Peter. Don't make a big thing out of it.'

'A ride home from where?'

She sighed. 'His daughter fell and hurt her ankle up in the meadow this morning, and I helped her home. After we took care of her, he offered to drive me home. I was tired from the long walk, and didn't want to bother you, so I accepted. OK?'

'Well . . .'

'And who is Julian Graves?' Charles asked lightly.

Laura laughed. 'He's our neighbour. Peter is furious at him because he's cutting down some dead old trees on his property.' She turned to her husband. 'Which is really too bad of him. He doesn't even know the man.'

'It's not just the trees, Laura, and you know it,' her husband protested.

Claudia stared at him. Was it possible that even Peter knew how the man had humiliated her? If he was aware of it, the whole village must be.

'What on earth are you talking about?' Laura asked mildly.

'Well, you remember that collision, the time Claudia ploughed into his truck? I called him to find out the damages, and he wouldn't even discuss it with me.'

'Oh!' Laura said with a laugh. 'The man's an artist. You know how temperamental artists are.'

'No, I don't, as a matter of fact. And even if I did, I don't see artistic temperament as an excuse for rudeness.'

Laura took him by the arm and led him towards the house and up the steps. 'I don't know what you're complaining about,' she said soothingly. 'If he doesn't want to collect for the damage Claudia did to his truck, I can't see that we're out anything.'

'That's right,' Charles said. 'In fact, I'd say you were ahead of the game.'

Still muttering about rudeness, Peter opened the front door and they all trooped inside. In the kitchen, Peter poured beer for Charles and himself while Laura put on a pot of coffee.

'How long can you stay, Charles?' Claudia asked him when they were seated around the table.

'Just overnight, I'm afraid,' he said with a rueful smile.

'Not another fishing trip, then, I take it?'

He shook his head. 'Afraid not. As a matter of fact, I really came to see you.' Claudia reddened and looked away. It had to be about the job, she thought miserably. She still hadn't come to any conclusion about that. 'But we can talk about that later,' Charles went on hastily. 'Perhaps I can talk you into showing me some of the sights of the island later this afternoon.'

Laura got up to pour out coffee for herself and Claudia. 'It's dreadful this time of year, I'm afraid. We're overrun with tourists.' She came back to the table and set down the mugs. 'Oh, I know,' she said, turning to Claudia. 'You could take Charles down to the small, sandy beach below the harbour. I don't think many of the holiday people have discovered it yet. They stick pretty much to their boats and the village streets.'

Claudia felt a sudden chill. She hadn't been back to that particular stretch of beach since the night she'd been there with Julian. She didn't want to go back now. She looked around the table at the others. They were all staring at her, waiting for her to speak and she thought quickly. It might be the perfect opportunity to exorcise the last remnants of the ghost.

'Yes,' she said. 'That sounds like a good idea. We can go right after lunch.'

CHAPTER SEVEN

'OH DEAR,' Claudia said. The crowd of people cluttering up the smooth stretch of beach was far worse than she had anticipated. She turned to Charles with a look of dismay. 'I'm afraid the tourists have discovered it, after all.'

'It doesn't matter. Come on, let's take a short walk. If we can't find a more private spot, we can always eat in the car.'

For the past two hours they had been driving leisurely around the entire circumference of the island, stopping occasionally at points of interest. Now Charles reached in the back seat to get the picnic meal Laura had pressed on them, over Claudia's objections, her eagerness to promote a romance with Charles so transparent as to be laughable.

They got out of the car and stood for a moment on the grass verge at the edge of the beach, the very spot where she and Julian had stopped that night. Anxious to obliterate every reminder of that awful night, Claudia glanced up and down the shoreline, looking for a more likely-looking spot to have their walk.

'If we go staight down past that large boulder,' she said, pointing, 'there's a more rocky stretch that won't be quite so popular.'

They began to pick their way carefully through the army of sunbathers. There were whole families, escaping from the cramped quarters of their boats for a day of swimming, and several closely intertwined young couples lying on their blankets in the more isolated spots.

As they made their way along the edge of the beach towards the boulder, the crowd thinned considerably, and by the time they skirted around it, the shore was deserted entirely, except for two or three solitary walkers who were more interested in keeping their footing over the rocks than they were in each other.

Can you manage this all right?' Charles asked, looking down dubiously at the treacherous terrain. 'I'm not sure I can.'

'Oh, I'm used to it. It's not so bad if you pay attention.'

'I wasn't raised in these parts, remember,' he said, taking her by the hand. 'You people are all half mountain goat.

They walked some distance along the curve of the rocky cliff above them until they finally came to an enormous outcropping of rock rising directly out of the sea, blocking their way entirely.

'It looks like the end of the road,' Charles said with a sigh of relief. 'I'm ready to quit.'

Claudia was just as glad to stop and rest. It had been a tiring day. They found a wide, flat rock near a clump of scrub pine and sat down gratefully on top of it, setting the picnic basket behind them in the shade.

Claudia leaned back against the trunk of a tree, stretched out her tired legs, and closed her eyes, letting the late afternoon sun beat down upon her. It was a still, windless day, and very quiet, with only the sound of the tide lapping against the shore and the occasional screeching of the gulls as they soared downwards from the top of the cliff.

When she opened her eyes again, the sun was dipping below the horizon, and it was growing cooler. She turned her head to see that Charles was still beside her, his eyes fastened upon her in a steady, intent gaze. She blinked, gave herself a little shake and sat up.

'I'm sorry, Charles,' she apologised. 'I must have dozed off.'

He smiled. 'No problem. I admit I grabbed a few winks myself. Besides,' he added, lowering his voice and putting a hand over hers, 'I like to look at you when you're asleep.'

She ran a hand self-consciously over her disordered hair. 'I'm afraid that's not such a lovely spectacle.'

His hand tightened. 'It is to me,' he said quietly. 'Are you hungry?'

'Not just yet.'

They sat in silence for a few moments, watching the sail-boats as they headed towards the harbour. Finally he spoke again. 'Claudia, I came up here today because I thought we ought to have a talk. When I was up here in May, I told you I wouldn't press you, not about the job, not about anything else. But it's been two months. You'll have to admit I've been patient.'

She turned and met his gaze. 'I do realise that,' she said. 'And I appreciate it. But I haven't come to a decision about the job. I just don't know if I'm ready to tackle that kind of responsibility yet—or if I could tolerate being around active dancers all the time.'

'I can understand that. There's still no hurry. The job is there whenever you want it.' He moved a little closer to her, so that his bare arm pressed against hers, and took her other hand. 'But that's not the most important reason I came. Claudia, you must know how I feel about you, how I've always felt about you.'

He hesitated, as though giving her the chance to stop him. She didn't know what to do. She'd expected something like this, even been a little afraid of it. The one thing she did know was that she owed it to this good, kind man to hear him out.

When she didn't say anything, he went on, 'I love you, Claudia. I'd like to put our relationship, our friendship, on a deeper level, to see you more often than once every few months. I guess that's the main reason I want you to take the job. Selfish of me, I know, but there it is. In time, if you learn to care for me, too, perhaps . . .' He broke off and frowned. 'I don't know. I'd marry you tomorrow, if you'd agree, but I know you wouldn't do that.'

'No,' she said softly. 'No, I wouldn't do that. I don't know if I ever want to marry. When I was dancing professionally, it was the furthest thing from my mind. You know how I feel about careers and marriage. Dancing always came first with me. Now everything is changed, and I'm still not used to it. Sometimes I think it would be lovely to marry, to have a home, raise a family.' She shrugged helplessly. 'At others, I just don't know.'

'I can appreciate that.' He thought a moment, then said, 'I do have one idea. You remember my sister, Helen?'

'Of course. She lives north of San Francisco up in Marin County. Sausalito, isn't it?'

He nodded. 'I've spoken to her, and she'd be delighted to have you come down and stay with her and her family for a week or two, or as long as you like. We could see each other more often that way, test the waters, so to speak, find out just how you feel.'

'I don't know, Charles,' she said slowly. 'Do you think it would be such a good idea to involve your family?'

'There's no involvement,' he said firmly. 'And no commitment, no strings. Call it a vacation, or a trial period, whatever you like. Just say you'll come.'

'When?'

'How about coming back with me tomorrow?' he replied promptly.

She smiled. 'Oh, no, I couldn't do that.' She thought a minute, then took a deep breath. 'How about September? After Labor Day.'

His face fell. 'That's over a month away!'

'I know, but I'd like to finish out the summer here. It may be my last time.'

'Well,' he said with a rueful smile. 'I guess it's better than nothing. September it is, then.'

Charles left the next day, and that evening Claudia was sitting out on the terrace, rocking slowly back and forth on the creaky old lawn swing, and thinking about the promise she had made to him, his declaration of love, the possibility of a future with him.

No matter how she tried to avoid it, however, thoughts of Julian Graves kept intruding, and she couldn't help comparing the two men. By virtually every reasonable standard, Charles always came out ahead as having the more admirable qualities. Julian was not only a cold, arrogant, self-centred monster, he was also haunted by some kind of black demon. Now that she was well on her way to conquering her own, she didn't need that.

Then she laughed aloud, as another more cogent

reason in Charles's favour struck her. He was available to her, while Julian definitely was not.

Just then she heard the back door close, footsteps, and Laura's voice came to her out of the shadows.

'Oh, there you are,' she said, and sat down beside her on the swing. 'What are you laughing about out here, all by yourself?'

'Oh, just me, I guess.'

They sat together in companionable silence for a while, rocking gently back and forth and listening to the squeak of the swing, the insects buzzing in the warm night air.

'I thought it might be because of Charles,' Laura said. When Claudia didn't answer, she added, 'He's obviously in love with you.'

Claudia turned and stared. 'How on earth do you know that?'

'Oh, my dear,' Laura said with a laugh, 'it's so obvious, even Peter caught it. But tell me, what are you going to do about it?'

'Nothing for now. I half promised to go stay with his sister in September for a week or two.'

'I see.' Laura settled herself more comfortably on the swing, then said casually, 'And what about Julian Graves?'

'Julian Graves?' Claudia could hardly believe her ears. 'What about him? Julian Graves is nothing to me. I detest the man. After what he did to me, I don't see how you can even suggest . . .'

'Hey, calm down,' Laura broke in. 'I'm sorry. I just thought that, since he brought you home yesterday, you might have patched things up.'

'Laura!' she cried. 'There was nothing *to* patch up.'

'He never even tried to explain why he behaved so

badly, then?' Laura asked mildly.

'Well . . .' Claudia faltered, her anger seeping away.

Laura raised a quizzical eyebrow. 'Well, what? Did he or didn't he?'

'Oh, he made a feeble stab at it,' Claudia mumbled.

'And?'

Claudia lifted her chin. 'I told him I wasn't interested in anything he had to say to me and to leave me alone.'

'I see. Do you think that was quite fair? Shouldn't you at least have given him a chance to explain his actions?'

'Fair? I'm under no obligation to be fair to Julian Graves! What was "fair" about the way he treated me? I don't care two pins for the man or his feeble explanations.'

'Then why the heated reaction?' Laura put a hand on her arm. 'Listen, Claudia, I'm not just being difficult. As a matter of fact, I'd be overjoyed to see you married to a man like Charles Thornton.' She paused. 'But there's something about Julian that tears at my heart. I feel so sorry for him.'

'Laura, I don't believe you're saying this. The man is a menace! He probably has a long string of other women he's seduced into believing him, trusting him, then dumped them the same way he did me as soon as his great artistic eye saw a flaw in them. Why, he even treats his own daughter like a stranger, an intruder.'

She stopped short as a swift image rose up in her mind of the haunted look in his eyes when Margaret was hurt. He had been terrified. And the way he'd held her, carried her, as though she were a precious jewel.

And then there was that portrait of the dancer she'd seen in his studio. In comparison with the bleak, muddy canvases surrounding it, it had been painted with a sense of joy, of hope, even of love, at least for what her dancing had once represented to him.

Could Laura be right? Was it possible she should have listened to him yesterday when he'd tried so hard to explain himself? Granted, she owed him nothing, but for her own sake, to rid herself of this destructive resentment, it might have helped. Perhaps, if he ever tried again, it might be wise at least to give him that chance.

'I don't think it matters, anyway,' she said at last. 'I'm quite certain I've seen the last of Julian Graves.'

But she was wrong. The very next day, as soon as Peter had gone back out to his sheep after lunch, the telephone rang. They were in the kitchen, clearing the dishes. Laura answered it, then handed the receiver to Claudia. 'It's for you,' she said, poker-faced, then hurried out of the room.

'Hello.'

'Claudia, it's Julian,' came his stiff voice. 'I apologise for intruding on you again this way, but Margaret has been nagging me all morning to call you and see if you'd consider coming over here for a short visit this afternoon.'

'How is she?' she asked, stalling.

'Restless,' was the grim reply. 'She's supposed to stay in bed for another week, then try getting around on crutches. It's only a minor sprain, and she's not in any more pain, but it's the very devil trying to keep her amused.' He paused for a moment, and when she didn't say anything, added, 'I know it's a lot to ask, and if it will reassure you, I've got a lot of work to do and intend to make myself scarce, but it would be a great favour to her—and to me—if you'd come. You wouldn't have to stay long.'

'I don't know,' she said slowly.

'You've made a tremendous hit with her,' he said quickly. 'She's lonely—I didn't realise how lonely until . . .' He broke off. 'Well, anyway, she's very taken with you, and it would mean a lot to her if you'd visit her.'

'Well, I'm fond of her, too. In fact, she reminds me a lot of myself at that age.'

'That doesn't surprise me. Will you come, then?'

'All right,' she said at last. 'When do you want me?'

'I can come over right away, if it would be convenient. I've pretty much exhausted my entertainment value already this morning, and would welcome a breather.'

'Give me about an hour, then, and I'll be ready.'

After they hung up, she stood with her hand on the receiver for several moments, pondering what she'd just done. Had she taken leave of her senses at last? Well, she could always get out of it, call him back and say she'd changed her mind. She certainly didn't owe him anything.

She was only going for Margaret's sake, she assured herself as she slowly climbed the stairs to her room. What over reason could there be?

She looked up to see Laura standing on the landing at the top of the stairs. There was a question in her eyes, a half-smile on her face, and Claudia reddened guiltily.

'Well?' Laura asked.

Claudia tossed her head. 'I've agreed to go over to visit Margaret for a little while this afternoon. I was just coming up to shower and change my clothes.'

'I see. That's nice. I'm sure she'll welcome the company, poor little thing.'

'Yes. She's a quiet, lonely little girl, and I've grown rather attached to her.'

Laura brushed past her on her way downstairs. 'Julian coming to pick you up?' she asked.

'Well, I can't very well walk.'

'No, of course not. I baked some cookies yesterday, chocolate chip. I'll pack some up for her.'

'That would be nice.'

After her shower, Claudia spent an agonising fifteen minutes trying to decide what to wear, until finally she grabbed the first thing in her wardrobe that came to hand, a pale blue cotton sundress that set off her tan nicely.

'Not that I care,' she muttered as she tugged it on over her head. 'It's not a date, for God's sake, and I don't have to impress anybody.

Still, she pinned her smooth, dark hair back a little more carefully than usual, and added some light eye make-up along with her usual trace of pale lipstick. There, she thought, smiling at her reflection in the mirror when she was done, that's not bad. She was really quite presentable—except for that awful leg. She raised her skirt and frowned down at it.

The scar had faded by now to an almost transparent white streak, the stitches virtually invisible, just as the doctors had promised her would happen in time. The hell with Julian Graves and his thirst for perfection, she said to herself, and went downstairs.

He arrived promptly, and this time he came into

the house. Peter was mercifully absent, but Laura fussed over him to a degree that turned Claudia's stomach, pressing cookies upon him and asking him the details of Margaret's injury.

When they were finally out in his car and on their way up the drive, Claudia breathed a sigh of relief. Then suddenly she became acutely conscious of the fact that she was alone with him again, and she shifted her weight away from him slightly.

The sharp grey eyes missing nothing; he darted a quick glance at her, then gave her a fleeting, sardonic smile and turned his eyes back on the road ahead.

He looked absolutely devastating today, his thick, black hair gleaming in the bright sunshine, his lean face deeply tanned. And when she met his eyes in that brief moment, the grey seemed so deep, so clear as to reach into the innermost depths of his being.

He was dressed casually in a pair of dark trousers and a thin blue shirt, the sleeves neatly rolled up above his elbows to reveal strong forearms, covered with silky dark hairs. His hands lay lightly on the steering wheel as he drove, large, competent hands with long, tapering fingers, an artist's hands, sensitive yet strong.

In spite of all Claudia's inner resistance, she was still powerfully attracted to the man, and much as she kept reminding herself of his arrogance, his cold, calculating heart, his cynical attitude, she couldn't quite fight down the recurring desire to reach out and touch those fine hands, to feel the rough cheek against hers, the wide, thin mouth . . .

Then she realised he'd been speaking to her.

'I'm sorry,' she said hastily. 'I didn't quite catch that.'

'Wool-gathering?' His white teeth flashed in a

quick, mocking smile.

'Something like that. What did you say?'

'I only asked if you had any brilliant ideas I could borrow to amuse Margaret during the next week.'

'I didn't think you planned to spend that much time with her,' she commented drily.

His heavy eyebrows contracted in a frown. 'You don't think much of me as a father, do you?'

She shrugged. 'Sorry. It's none of my business.'

'Well, you might be right,' he said with a sigh. 'What I know about small girls could be summed up in about one sentence.'

She gave him a grudging smile. 'And what's that?'

'They're nothing like boys,' he stated with feeling.

They were at his house now. It was quite different from her brother's more traditional place, which was wood-framed and painted white with dark green shutters.

Julian's house was low and sprawling and built of buff-coloured stucco or adobe, in a rather Spanish-looking style. A long, covered walkway with a black wrought-iron railing ran along the entire front. Bright red flowers bloomed in the small garden.

The house was shaded by several large cherry trees, and the noise of the birds twittering in the topmost branches as they decimated the ripening fruit was almost deafening.

'Watch out where you walk,' Julain said, as Claudia got out of the car and stepped on to the brick paving. He took her lightly by the arm. 'The ground is covered with half-eaten cherries the birds have dropped.'

The touch of his hand on her bare skin was like a sudden charge of electricity. 'I can manage,' she said stiffly, and pulled her arm away.

His face hardened as his hand dropped to his side, but he only murmured, 'Of course.'

Inside, the blinds were closed against the afternoon sun, and the house was cool and dim. On their way down the hall to Margaret's bedroom, they passed by the large, immaculate kitchen, and Julian pointed inside.

'Make yourself at home,' he said. 'There's still some coffee on the stove, but if you want to make a fresh pot, please do. Mrs Jacobs made lemonade yesterday, which should still be drinkable, or there's beer, wine, soft drinks, if you prefer.'

'How about tea?' she asked with a mischievious smile.

He nodded. 'That, too.'

At the door to Margaret's room, he stopped and called inside, 'Well, here she is.' Then he turned and looked down at Claudia. 'I'll leave you two females alone, then,' he said briefly. 'If you need me, I'll be in my studio. It's the last door at the end of the corridor.'

With that, he turned and sauntered away from her, every inch the master of the house, his gait unhurried and assured. Claudia looked after him for a moment, then turned and went in to Margaret's bedroom.

By five o'clock, Claudia had read aloud every book in sight, exhausted her store of card games, and was frantically searching her mind for entertainment possibilities, when she noticed that Margaret's eyes were growing heavy. She sat still, watching, until they closed at last, and the deep, heavy breathing told her the girl was asleep.

She got up from the chair by the side of the bed and tiptoed slowly out of the room into the corridor.

There was no sign of life, not a sound to be heard except the slow ticking of a clock in another room and the muffled racket of the birds coming from the cherry tree outside.

She stretched widely, cramped from the hours of sitting still, and wandered down to the kitchen to make herself a cup of tea. It was time she was getting home, but where was Julian? When her tea was ready, she took it over to the round oak table in a corner of the room and sat down to drink it.'

Although the time she'd spent with the restless, bed-ridden Margaret had been taxing, she'd enjoyed the visit. There was something very soothing about the house, too, its quiet, its serenity, its distinctively masculine flavour. There was a slightly brooding quality about it, too, that was not unpleasant. In fact, it seemed somehow appropriate, a reflection of its owner's personality.

She had just finished her tea, and was wondering if she should go look for Julian, when he suddenly appeared at the door.

'I see the invalid is finally asleep,' he remarked as he strolled inside. 'Was it terribly boring for you?'

'Not at all. Although I'll have to admit I was just about at my wits' end when she did drift off.'

'Are you finding everything you need?' he asked politely. 'I see you did make yourself tea.'

'Yes.' She hesitated. 'Would you like a cup?'

'No, thanks. As a matter of fact, I was thinking more along the lines of a gin and tonic. Would you join me?'

She started to get up from the table. 'I don't think

so. It's probably time I was getting home.'

He crossed over to a cabinet and took down a bottle of gin. 'Is there something pressing waiting for you at home?' he called over his shoulder. He went to the refrigerator, but before he opened it, he turned to her. 'Like that strange man who was waiting for you at your place the other day?'

She laughed. 'Strange man? You mean Charles Thornton? He's hardly a stranger.'

He mixed his drink, raised the glass to his mouth and gave her a narrow-eyed look over the rim. 'Well, he is to me. You're close, then? It certainly looked that way.' He put his head back and took a long swallow of his drink.

'Close enough,' she replied non-committally. She watched, entranced, unable to tear her eyes from the working of the long column of his throat as he swallowed. She stood up. 'I really think . . .'

'I'd like to show you my studio before you go,' he said abruptly. He set his glass down on the counter and wiped his mouth with the back of his hand.

She thought for a minute. There was no need to mention the fact that Margaret had already shown it to her the day she had fallen. 'All right,' she said at last.

They walked together down the entire length of the hall, and went inside the cavernous room. Today she noticed that the blinds were open. The absence of trees on that side of the house let in a strong north light, essential, she knew, for a painter.

It was just as she remembered it, the subdued violence of the stark paintings just as disturbing. They walked around the room silently for a little while, stopping before each canvas, until they came to the easel that was set up so that the light would fall over his shoulder. The half-finished painting upon it was so entirely different from the others that she turned to him in surprise.

'I see you've changed your style quite dramatically.'

He shrugged. 'That happens from time to time. All artists go through different stages. It's the only way they grow. Otherwise they remain stagnant. What do you think?'

'You mean, which do I prefer?'

He nodded. The painting on the easel was a still life done in a somewhat abstract form, but the blue bowl of fruit and the tall vase of flowers in the foreground were still recognisable. It was the colour that was such a marked contrast to his earlier work—bright clear reds and yellows, greens and blues, that glowed with life.

'There's no question,' she said at last, pointing at the easel. 'In my untutored view, this is far more appealing.'

He gave her an enigmatic smile. 'The others have made a lot of money for me.'

'Money isn't always an indication of quality.'

'No, perhaps not. But it can give one the freedom to pursue quality.'

'Is that what you've done?'

'Not intentionally. Like most painters I know, I pretty much work in the dark and follow my instincts. When I painted those,' he said with a sweeping gesture towards the darker canvases, 'I felt that way. They were a reflection of my state of mind, if you will. Luckily, people wanted to buy them. Now . . .' He broke off with a shrug. 'Well, we'll just have to wait and see. My agent seems to think the new ones will do just as well.'

The lovely Sharon, Claudia thought, and watched him as he walked over to the windows and pulled the blinds closed, shutting out the bright light and casting the studio in dimness. She wanted badly to ask him about the portrait of the dancer she had seen that day, but didn't quite have the nerve. She knew too that she should go, but there was something mesmerising about the darkened room, the smell of turpentine, the stark paintings hanging on the walls, and she felt unable to move.

When he came back to her, he stood some distance away, looking down at her, a strange, far-away look in his eyes, as though he was debating inwardly with himself. His eyes were half closed and he was turned towards the window, which threw faint streaks of light across his features through the slats of the blinds. She couldn't quite make out his expression.

Finally, he spoke, his voice low. 'I wonder if you'd give me that chance now to explain my actions to you.'

Suddenly, Claudia was frightened. 'Oh, Julian . . .' she began.

'Five minutes,' he said. 'That's all I ask.'

'Julian, it doesn't matter, honestly it doesn't. I don't bear you any ill will, and I don't want to be your enemy. Let the past lie.'

His face darkened. 'I cannot bear it,' he ground out, 'that you have such a low opinion of me! I'm not claiming I'm a saint. I've by no means lived like a monk since my wife died. But I've always tried to be honest in my relations with women, and knowing how miserably I failed to do that with you, of all people, simply torments me.'

She whirled around, turning away from him, unable to look at the haggard, haunted face another moment. 'All right, all right,' she said at last. 'Go ahead. I'll listen. But it won't make any difference.'

She waited, her eyes closed, her hands clenched into fists, for the hateful reminder of that awful night. Julian didn't say anything for a long time, and when he began to speak his voice was so low as to be almost inaudible.

'The first thing I think you should know,' he said, 'is that the reason I didn't show up the day after we went out for dinner as I'd promised was definitely *not* because I was turned off by the knowledge that your accident had left you with a permanent injury. I know it looked that way, and I don't blame you for thinking that. It was entirely my fault.'

She turned around slowly and raised her head to glare fiercely into his eyes. 'How can you expect me to believe that?' she said bitterly. 'Everything you did, every word you uttered before I told you led me to believe that—that . . .'

'That I was strongly attracted to you? That I wanted to make love to you?' he said in a flat tone. 'Well, you were right, that's exactly how it was.'

'But you couldn't bear the thought of a love affair with a cripple,' she bit out.

'No!' he shouted. 'That's what I'm trying to tell you.' He shook his head wearily, and rubbed a hand over the back of his neck. 'It wasn't that. That would have made no difference to me.'

'Well, *what*, then?' she cried. 'What else is there?'

'It was the accident itself, the way it happened. When you told me what had caused your injury, I just lost it and ran.'

'I don't understand.'

'No, I don't blame you. Maybe you will, though, when I tell you that my wife died in the same way. And,' he added grimly, 'I killed her.'

CHAPTER EIGHT

CLAUDIA'S head was spinning. She stared at him, open-mouthed. 'You killed your wife?' she finally managed to croak out. Mrs Jacobs had said the same thing, but she'd put it down to sensational exaggeration.

'Oh, it wasn't murder, not in the technical sense,' he went on in a dull tone. 'But the hell of it is I'll never know whether it was an accident or whether I did it intentionally.'

'But what happened?'

He raised his head and gazed at her with pain-filled eyes. 'I was driving the car the night of the accident. We were on our way home from a party—we were living in San Francisco then—it was raining, we'd both been drinking. As usual, we were arguing. Then it just happened. I took a corner too fast, the car went out of control, and . . .' He broke off and looked away.

She shivered a little. 'That's terrible, Julian. But it could have happened to anybody. You didn't do it deliberately.'

With the raise of an eyebrow, his mouth curled in a bitter self-mocking smile. 'Didn't I? I'll never be sure of that. You see, I wanted to be free of her. We'd discussed divorce many times, but always put it off because of Margaret. We didn't have a real marriage in any sense. I managed to be away a lot.' He paused for a moment, then continued, 'And while I was away, she amused herself with a variety of other men, a few of my own friends among them.'

'I'm so sorry, Julian,' she said weakly. 'But I still don't understand what that had to do with me.'

'I'll try to explain. That night when we had dinner together, when you told me you'd been injured in the same way, all the old guilt came back, choking me. I had to get out of there, away from you, away from any reminder of that awful night. I could still hear her screaming, still see the blood, the body crushed under the car.' He paused, then said dully, 'It wasn't a good marriage, but I loved her once, and I certainly didn't want her dead. At least, not consciously.'

Claudia didn't know what to say. If he'd been living with that load of guilt all these months, she could understand why he'd reacted so violently when she'd told him about her own accident. It must have brought back all the painful memories, all the things he wanted to forget.

He raised his head again and looked into her eyes, holding them in his. 'I was attracted to you right from the beginning,' he said softly. 'In fact, I used to sneak brief glimpses of you from a distance way last winter as you worked on your side of that wall.' He laughed shortly. 'I didn't pay much attention, though. I was too hellbent on cutting down all those trees. It was a form of therapy, I guess. I had to take my anger and guilt out on something. Then the day you fell and I really got a close look at you for the first time, that lovely, smooth, dark hair, the wonderful fragile bones, your slight body like a feather in my arms . . .'

Claudia could hardly breathe. The very air felt like a weight on her, suffocating her. It was all clear now.

He wasn't repelled by her. She didn't need to fight him any more, fight her own overpowering attraction to him. She could love him again.

'Julian,' she whispered, and moved a step closer to him, ready to fall into his arms.

But his hands remained stiffly at his sides, and he scowled darkly at her. 'This is not something I talk about, Claudia, not ever, not to any other human being. I only told you because I couldn't live with myself knowing I'd hurt you.' He raised one hand in a gesture of defeat. 'So that while it's important to me that you understand, that you don't despise me, in the long run it's probably just as well that nothing ever started up between us.'

She took a step backwards and put a hand to her throat. 'What do you mean?'

'That whole experience, the bad marriage, the accident, my wife's death, all had a profound and irreversible impact on me. I vowed even before she died that I would never, under any circumstances whatsoever, take that kind of chance again. I couldn't paint for months after she died, and my work means everything to me.'

'I see,' she said quietly. 'But you said yourself that you haven't lived like a monk. That doesn't quite make sense—or am I missing something?'

He smiled thinly. 'I'm thirty-seven years old, not quite senile yet, and I like beautiful women.'

'You mean women without limps and scars?' she said. 'Is that it?'

'No!' he ground out. 'That's not it. I mean women who don't want a commitment any more than I do. And if there's one thing that comes through loud and clear about you, Claudia Hamilton, it's that you're not that kind of woman.'

'And just how do you know that?'

His eyes flew open at that, and Claudia felt a warm rush of satisfaction. She'd surprised him at last, broken through that thick shell of certainty about who she was and what she could tolerate. He cocked his head to one side and gazed at her thoughtfully.

'Are you telling me I was wrong about you?' he said in a tone of disbelief. 'If you expect me to swallow any stories about your lurid past, or a long string of love affairs, I'll tell you right now it just won't wash. I admit I know very little about the inner workings of the female mind, but I couldn't possibly be that wrong about you.'

She reddened and looked down at her feet. 'All right. I won't even try to do that.' Then she raised her head and gave him a defiant look. 'But my life changed irrevocably, too, you know, when this happened.' She pointed down at her leg. 'My work was everything to me, too. Now that's gone, I have to find something to replace it.

'And what about the guy? Charles, I think you said his name was. Is he part of your remodelling plan?'

'I don't know. I doubt it.'

'Does he love you?'

'He says he does.'

'Want to marry you?'

'Probably, in time.'

He gave her a searching glance. 'How old are you, Claudia? Twenty-five, twenty-six?'

'I'm twenty-seven. What difference does that make?'

'Take my advice, and marry your Charles,' he said with firm conviction. 'I sympathise with you that your career is over, probably more than anyone except another artist could, but life is not over for you. You're still young enough and untouched enough to believe in fairy-tales. You can still make a home, have children, perhaps even live happily ever after. But only with the right kind of man.'

'And in your expert opinion, Charles Thornton is that kind of man?'

'That's right.' He smiled. 'And you're angry with me again, aren't you?'

'A little. I don't especially like the way you've planned my life out for me. I'd rather like to do that myself.' She narrowed her eyes at him. 'To tell you the truth, Julian Graves, what I really think is that not only do you not know the first thing about me, you also don't even know yourself very well.' She smoothed her dress down and turned from him. 'Now, I think I'd like to go home.'

She started stalking out of the room with as much dignity as her bad leg allowed, her back stiff and straight, literally rigid with indignation. But, before she could reach the door, she heard him call to her, 'Claudia. Wait!' She stopped short and listened to his footsteps coming up behind her. Then his hands settled firmly on her shoulders, and he turned her around to face him.

'Look at me,' he said gruffly. She raised her eyes to meet his. 'Are you telling me,' he went on, 'that in spite of everything I've told you today, you're crazy enough to imagine you want to get involved with a man like me? A man who has absolutely nothing to offer you?'

At that moment she wasn't sure what she thought, but she did know quite well what she wanted. She wanted those warm, strong hands to remain on her shoulders for ever. She wanted to drown in those speckled grey eyes. And, most of all, she wanted to feel that fine mouth pressing against hers.

'Oh, Julian,' she said with a sigh. 'Haven't we talked enough already? I'm a big girl. Let me be the judge of what's good or bad for me.'

His hands tightened on her shoulders. He scowled down at her, then sighed and pulled her to him. His arms came around her and he stood perfectly still, his face against her hair, for several moments. Then he lifted his head and gazed down at her.

'Are you sure you know what you're doing?' he asked slowly.

She nodded. 'I know.'

'I don't want to hurt you, Claudia. Not in any way.'

She put a finger on his lips. 'Listen, Julian. If my accident taught me anything at all, it's that it's important to taste all of life's joys before it's too late. I wanted to die when I found out I'd never dance again. Now I don't. It's that simple.'

He put both his hands on her face, leaned down and kissed her lightly on the mouth. His lips began to glide over hers in a slow, sensuous movement that set her blood racing, her heart pounding. As the slow heat began to build inside her, she pressed herself up against him, all along the length of his hard, lean body. His arms tightened around her, and as his mouth opened slightly over hers he made a low sound deep in his throat.

Just then, through the open door, came the sound of a small voice. 'Daddy? Claudia? Where are you?'

With a little groan, Julian tore his mouth away and stood back from her, still breathing hard and staring at her with glazed eyes. He kneaded her shoulders gently and heaved a regretful sigh.

Then he smiled and said, 'How are you at Monopoly?'

By the time he drove her home that night, Claudia was floating on a cloud and felt as though she'd died and gone to heaven. They'd spent the remainder of the evening entertaining Margaret and, although the haunted look in Julian's eyes never really left him, he seemed to be enjoying himself.

When she'd called Laura late that afternoon to tell her she wouldn't be home for dinner, Laura hadn't said anything, but several unasked questions had virtually crackled along the telephone wire. They'd had a light supper together in Margaret's bedroom, then Mrs Jacobs had come to sit with the girl while Julian took Claudia home.

They spoke very little on the way. There was a full moon in the dark blue night sky, casting its pale glow on Julian's face as he drove along, and she couldn't get enough of looking at him. He seemed preoccupied, serious, his thin mouth set in a straight line, his forehead faintly furrowed. She knew him well enough by now not to question him or force conversation, and the silence was not uneasy.

He drew up in front of the house, switched off the motor, pulled on the handbrake, then sat motionless in his seat for a while, staring out the front windscreen. It was still very early, not quite nine o'clock. Inside the house, the living-room lights were still burning.

'Would you like to come inside?' she asked quietly.

He turned to her and smiled. 'I don't think that's such a good idea,' he said drily. 'I'm not exactly your brother's favourite person, you know.'

'Oh, don't mind Peter. He's so much older than I am—fifteen years—that he's always thought it his duty to be over-protective.'

'That's quite a gap in age. You must have been rather a surprise to your parents.'

'I suppose so. I never really thought much about it. They were both killed in a boating accident when I was only thirteen. Peter and Laura were married by then, and they actually raised me. How about you? Do you have any family?'

'Just the one sister, and we're not close. My father was an army officer, and we lived in posts all over the world. I guess I got used to being rootless, sort of a perpetual nomad. My mother hated it. She used to talk about the day when he would retire and she could have a real home at last. Then she died of cancer during his last year. Ironic, isn't it?'

'What happened to your father?'

'He died shortly afterwards,' he said vaguely, and his face got that closed-in look again.

He lit a cigarette, and Claudia sat quietly beside him while he smoked in silence. She didn't know what to do. She wasn't used to his strange moods, and would have to learn when he wanted to be with her and when he wanted to be alone.

Finally she put her hand on the door and said, 'Well, if you're sure you don't want to brave Peter, I'd probably better get inside.'

He ground out his cigarette in the ashtray and turned to her. 'Don't go just yet.'

He put his arm along the back of her seat, then lowered it around her shoulders and pulled her head down against his chest. With his other hand he stroked her hair. She could hear the slow, steady beat of his heart under her ear, and smell his clean, masculine fragrance.

'I don't ever want to hurt you, Claudia,' he said finally in a low voice. 'I've tried to be honest with you about how I feel, but I'm not sure you really understand what you're letting yourself in for.'

She lifted her head and raised her face to his. 'Please, let's not get into that again. I know exactly what I'm doing.'

He gazed down at her in the moonlight, a quirky smile on his face. Then his other arm came around her and he placed his mouth over hers in a long kiss, both tender and sensuous at the same time. When she felt his tongue rasp lightly over her lips, she parted them instinctively.

He shifted his position slightly so that he was leaning over her, the weight of his body pushing her back against the seat. One hand came up to cover her breast, the long fingers playing lightly on the bare skin beneath the low-cut bodice of her dress, and the kiss deepened.

Claudia felt as though she was drowning. The sensations aroused in her by his mouth, his hands, his long, hard body pressing against hers, were overpowering in their intensity. She gave herself up to him completely, and would have agreed to anything he asked of her at that moment.

Then he broke off his kiss and moved away from her. 'You'd better get inside,' he said roughly, 'before it's too late.'

She shivered a little as he withdrew, but she knew he was right. The front seat of a car was no place to make love.

He walked with her to the door and gave her another long, lingering kiss. 'I'll call you tomorrow,' he said, and turned to go. When he was half-way down the steps of the porch, he turned around. 'And this time you can count on it.'

She slipped quietly inside the house, hoping to sneak up the stairs to her room before Laura or Peter could confront her, but as soon as she closed the door noiselessly behind her she turned to see her brother standing in the hall, his arms crossed in front of his chest, his legs apart, and a decidedly hostile expression on his face.

'What was that all about?' he asked grimly.

'Nothing,' she said defensively. 'Julian just brought me home, that's all. I've been visiting his daughter.'

'For seven hours?' he growled, tapping his watch.

Claudia had had enough. She raised her chin and stated firmly, 'Now, listen here, Peter Hamilton. I'm not a teenager you can boss around, I'm a grown woman, and what I do is none of your business.'

'It is while you're in my house.'

'Well, then, maybe I'd better leave *your* house.'

Their eyes locked together for a full minute, neither of them giving way an inch. Claudia was so angry by now that she was ready to march upstairs and pack her bags that very night, except that she didn't have any place to go. The one hotel was always full in the summer, and she didn't even have transport.

Just then, Laura appeared in the doorway. She took one look at the little tableau before her and made a noise of disgust.

'Just look at the two of you!' she exclaimed, marching towards them. 'Peter, you should be ashamed of yourself. What Claudia does is her own business. And it's her home, too, remember. Really, I can't believe you!'

Peter's gaze faltered, and he frowned uncertainly

at his wife. 'Don't tell me you approve of her taking up with that madman.'

'Madman?' Laura cried. 'What on earth are you talking about? He's a perfectly respectable man. You're just mad at him because he cut down the trees, and you know it.' She sighed deeply, gave Claudia a sympathetic look of female complicity, and led her husband back in the direction of the living-room. 'Come on now, Peter,' she soothed, 'I'll fix you a nice cup of tea and we can talk about it calmly.'

When they were gone and out of earshot, Claudia had to smile. She was still irritated with her brother's high handed manner, but in her heart she knew quite well—as Laura did—that his only real motive was her welfare. What Peter didn't understand, she thought as she slowly made her way upstairs, was that even he couldn't protect her against falling in love. It either happened or it didn't, and no amount of warning, whether from Peter or Laura or even Julian himself, could alter the way she felt.

Julian did call her the next morning, right after breakfast, as he'd promised. His first words to her, after they'd said hello, were, 'Well, have you changed your mind yet?'

'About what?'

'About me. About us.'

'No, of course not. I told you I wouldn't.'

'Well, I'm glad. I figured after you'd had a chance to sleep on it you'd realise what a foolish step it would be to get involved with a man like me.'

Claudia lowered her voice. She was at the telephone in the hall, not far from the ktichen where Peter and Laura were still finishing their coffee. 'I happen to be rather taken with a man just like you,' she murmured.

There was a short silence. Then he said, 'Would it bore you too much to spend the day here with Margaret and me? It's Sunday, and Mrs Jacobs is adamant about not working on the Sabbath.'

'Not at all. But I'm going to see if I can find some of my old games. I'm really rather sick of Monopoly.'

He laughed. 'That's because Margaret beat us both so badly.'

'Could be.'

'All right, then. I'll see you—when? In about an hour?'

'That's fine.'

After they hung up, she went upstairs to the unused bedroom down the hall from hers, where Laura had stored her old toys and games. It wasn't until she got inside and switched on the light that she remembered it was also the room where her old full-length mirror had been banished. There it was, directly in front of her.

She gazed at her reflection. That morning had dawned bright and warm, and she'd put on an old pair of shorts and a sleeveless knit shirt that left her arms and legs bare. She walked slowly towards the mirror, and stared in amazement. Today she saw an entirely different person from the one who'd stood there three months ago, so thin and gaunt, in the depths of depression.

The scar was still there, of course. It always would be. And so was the limp. She could never dance again, nor would she ever win any bathing-beauty contests. But that wasn't what she wanted, anyway. Even dancing took second place now to her love of Julian, and the thrill of performing before an audience couldn't come close to what she felt in his arms.

As she thought of Julian, a sudden cold chill passed over her, marring her happiness. He had made it abundantly clear that, whatever relationship they entered into, it would not be permanent, that there was to be no commitment, implied or stated. Could she live with that?

'Yes,' she said aloud to her reflection. 'I can. I will. I must.' Life was too short to plan ahead. You had to seize whatever happiness you could find, whenever it offered itself. It might never come again.

The next month passed so quickly that Claudia could hardly believe it was already almost September. Soon the summer would be over, the tourists would leave, and they'd have the island to themselves again.

She'd seen Julian almost every day in that short month, and her cup of joy was truly filled to the brim and running over. Even Peter had finally accepted that Julian was an important part of her life now, and had come to agree, albeit grudgingly, that he wasn't so bad after all, now that he'd put away his axe.

They did everything together, swam, drove, hiked, sailed, but what she enjoyed most was the quiet time at his house with just the three of them, having a barbecue on the patio, picnicking in the woods or on the beach, or just playing one of the games she'd unearthed.

His lovemaking remained ardent, but restrained. He always held back, checking himself when things threatened to get out of hand, just as though he were protecting her from herself. Besides, Margaret was always in the house, and they had to be circumspect for her sake.

The girl's ankle was all healed by now, and she'd gone back to her dancing lessons with enthusiasm.

One night, when the three of them were having dinner in Julian's kitchen, Margaret announced that her dancing classes was going on a weekend trip to the Rosario resort on Orcas Island that Friday.

'Can I go, Daddy?' she asked. 'I already said I could.'

Julian raised his head and looked at Claudia. As their eyes met, she could read the unasked question in his quite clearly. She smiled and gave a slight, imperceptible nod.

Julian turned to his daughter. 'Sure you can go. What will you need to take with you?'

When Julian came to pick her up late Friday afternoon after dropping Margaret off at the boat dock, she was all ready for him. She'd packed toothbrush and a change of underwear in her handbag, and while she waited for him she told Laura not to expect her home that night.

Laura only gave her a mild look. 'All right,' she said quietly. 'Are you sure you know what you're doing?'

Claudia laughed. 'No. I only know I have to do it.'

At Julian's they had dinner, then he told her he had something he wanted to show her in his studio. When they got there, he switched on a small lamp attached to the top of the easel which was standing in the middle of the room. Claudia caught her breath at what she saw. There, propped on the easel, was the portrait of the nude dancer. It was finished now, and the beauty and grace of the delicate figure was astounding.

She turned to Julian. 'Is that how you see me?'

He nodded. 'Yes.' He took a step toward her. 'As an artist and as a man.'

She held her breath, waiting, and in the next moment he made a low sound deep in his throat and gathered her into his arms. His open mouth covered hers in a searing, probing kiss.

Then he jerked his head back suddenly. 'I want you, Claudia,' he rasped.

'Yes,' she said, and raised her arms around his neck, running her fingers up into the thick hair.

His mouth came down on hers again, and his strong teeth pressed against her lips hard. His hands were moving up and down her back, sliding the thin material of her sundress over her skin. Then one hand came around her waist, over her ribcage, and settled on her breast.

With his mouth still on hers, Julian drew one strap of her dress down over her shoulder and, with a sensuous, gliding motion, his hand dipped beneath the low neckline to touch her bare skin. She could feel the tips of her breasts hardening under his sensitive fingers as he made delicate circles around first one taut peak, then the other.

As his fingers worked their magic, she let her head fall back, moaning aloud at the thrilling sensations he aroused in her. Suddenly, he left her and pulled back. He stood there panting, his half-closed eyes hooded, his black hair falling over his forehead.

'Are you sure, Claudia?' he breathed.

She only smiled and nodded. He put an arm around her then, and led her over to the screen in one corner of the room. Behind it was a low couch. He stood beside it for a moment, as though waiting for her to object, but when she stayed perfectly still he sat down on it, pulling her with him.

He reached out to remove the pins from her long, silky hair and combed his fingers through it carefully until it fell over her shoulders and down her back. Then he pulled both straps of her dress over her arms until the bodice lay loosely around her waist.

His eyes travelled over her. 'You're even more beautiful than I imagined,' he said softly. 'The painting doesn't begin to do you justice.'

He ran his large hands up from her waist to her shoulders, then clutched at her face. Placing his mouth on hers, he slowly lowered her down on the couch.

When Claudia awoke some time later, it was dark outside the window and the dim light above the easel was still burning.

She raised herself up on her elbows and looked down at the sleeping man beside her, listening to his deep, steady breathing and watching the rise and fall of his bare chest. Their bodies were still touching, and he lay with one hand flung over his head.

His hair was mussed, giving him a boyish look, and the harsh lines of his face were smoothed in sleep. His chin was raised slightly to reveal the long column of his throat. The skin of his broad shoulders and muscled chest looked smooth and tanned, and there was a sharp line just below his waist where it whitened.

He was so beautiful, she thought, just like the David of Michelangelo. Then a sudden, deep sadness pierced her heart. It had been so perfect. He'd been so gentle, so sensitive to her needs, her wishes. But not once, not even during the height of his passion and adoration of her body, had he spoken one word of love.

It was daylight the next time she opened her eyes, and Julian was gone. From the kitchen she could smell bacon cooking and the faint aroma of fresh coffee.

Claudia sat up, yawned and stretched widely, then heard his footsteps coming down the hall towards her. Realising she didn't have a stitch on, she pulled the sheet up to cover her nakedness. In a minute he appeared at the door, freshly showered and shaved, his dark hair still damp. He had on a pair of khaki shorts and nothing else.

He smiled at her. 'Good morning, Sleeping Beauty.' He came to sit beside her on the couch and gave her a searching look. 'How are you?'

'Wonderful,' she replied happily. 'Hungry, though.'

He frowned slightly. 'I had no idea it ws the first time for you,' he said in a deadly serious tone. 'How in the world did you manage that?'

'Oh, I was saving myself for you,' she said with a little laugh. She tossed the long hair out of her eyes. 'And also too busy dancing. Does it matter?'

'No. I guess not, not if it doesn't matter to you.' He leaned over to kiss her bare shoulder. 'You have ten minutes to shower and dress before breakfast,' he said sternly.

'My,' she said playfully and batted her eyes at him, 'you mean you're actually going to cook for me?'

He eyed her narrowly. 'Keep looking at me like that and we may never eat again.'

'Like what?' she said, all wide-eyed innocence. She fluttered her eyelashes at him again.

A familiar gleam appeared in the grey eyes. In one swift movement he had reached out a hand and whipped away the sheet that covered her. She sat motionless under his penetrating gaze, and felt the slow heat building in her again. Then he rose to his feet, and she watched, mesmerised, as his hands moved slowly to the waistband of his shorts.

CHAPTER NINE

THE breakfast was cold by the time they got around to it, and while Julian cooked another one Claudia finally took her shower. Alone in the large tiled bathroom, she looked around with interest at Julian's personal belongings, all the masculine objects set out on the counter, his still-damp towel hanging on the rack.

Unlike most artistic types she knew, Julian appeared to be almost obsessively neat. The towel and washcloth were folded carefully, the cap firmly screwed on to the tube of toothpaste, the shaving gear laid out with precision. The room even smelled like Julian, of his particular brand of soap, a faint, lingering aroma of tobacco.

When she'd finished, she went into the kitchen. Julian was just laying out their meal on the round oak table near the corner windows. It was a foggy, rather overcast day, the sun obscured by thin wisps of low clouds, and Claudia shivered a little in her thin sundress.

'Are you cold?' he asked, watching her.

'A little. What happened to our sun?'

He glanced out of the window. 'It looks as though it might rain. So much for our picnic.'

'Maybe you'd like to get some work done today,' she suggested.

He smiled at her. 'Maybe. We'll see. I'd try to talk you into posing for me, but I'm afraid if you did I wouldn't get much painting done.' He set their plates on the table. 'Sit down. I'm going to get you something to put over your shoulders.'

She sat at the table sipping her orange juice, and when he came back he had one of his plaid work shirts with him. As he placed it around her shoulders, he bent down to kiss her on the neck. She twisted her head so that his lips landed on the corner of her mouth, and his hands moved to her breast.

Just then there came the sound of a car pulling into the drive. Julian straightened up, listening. 'Expecting company?' Claudia asked, and Julian shook his head.

Then they heard the car door slam and the tap, tap of high heels approaching. There was a light knock on the door, it opened and a woman stepped inside. Claudia stared. It was the tall blonde who had been with Julian in the village the day of the collision.

'Julian, did you get my——' she called brightly. Then she faltered. 'Oh,' she said, and her eyes swept over the room, first to Julian, then to Claudia, and back to Julian again, a question in her flashing green eyes. 'Pardon me. Am I interrupting something?'

'Hello, Sharon,' Julian said easily. He walked over to her, leaned down and kissed her lightly on the forehead. 'I wasn't expecting you until tomorrow.'

She pouted up at him prettily and reached out a hand to flick an imaginary piece of dust off his shirt, then took him by the arm. 'Didn't you get my letter? I told you I could make it a day early.' Her gaze shifted past him to Claudia, still sitting motionless at the breakfast table. 'I tried to call you, but you didn't answer.'

'I was in the studio. I can't hear the telephone in there.'

Claudia was paralysed. She knew her face must be flaming by now, but she was trapped and would just have to brazen it out the best she could.

As she watched them, noticing particularly the possessive way the woman clung to Julian's arm, her embarrassment at being caught with Julian like this gradually gave way to a sickening wrench in the pit of her stomach. It was bad enough to sit there and watch another woman *touching* him, but far worse that it should be a woman as glamorous and sophisticated as this one.

She was tall, much taller than Claudia, who barely reached five feet six, and her golden hair was arranged in an impeccable cut that produced a shaggy, casual effect, but which Claudia knew was the result of the most expensive styling. She was wearing a beautifully cut pair of green linen trousers, just the colour of her eyes, and a white sweater that did nothing to hide the slim figure underneath. A matching green jacket was slung loosely over her shoulders.

'Claudia,' Julian said, turning to her, 'this is Sharon Quarles, my agent. Sharon, Claudia Hamilton. She's a neighbour.'

A neighbour? Claudia could hardly believe her ears. A sudden fierce sense of outrage rose up in her, almost choking her, a feeling she recognised instantly as blind, unreasoning jealousy.

She felt one minute like a dowdy frump, sitting there in her old sundress with Julian's shirt around her shoulders, and the next like a cheap tramp, a one-night stand, a *neighbour*, for God's sake, who had just happened to spend the night in Julian's bed, someone for him to fill in time while he waited for Sharon.

As they came towards her, Claudia noticed that Sharon didn't walk so much as glided sinuously. Her make-up was perfect, just enough to give nature a helping hand, but laid on so carefully and expertly that it was unnoticeable as make-up at all. Claudia could cheerfully have scratched her fingernails down those smooth cheeks, and she had a mental vision of the bloody tracks they would leave.

They sat down at the table, and immediately became deeply involved in a discussion about Julian's upcoming exhibit. With every nerve-end screaming, Claudia lowered her eyes to her plate and began stuffing in the food Julian had cooked for her and which now tasted like nothing more than dry chunks of cardboard.

When she had finally choked down the last mouthful of bacon and eggs and drained her cold cup of coffee, she rose to her feet with as much dignity as she could muster and gazed down at them.

'Excuse me,' she interrupted.

Julian broke off in mid-sentence and gave her an enquiring look, but without another word she turned on her heel and *made* herself walk slowly away from the table.

'Claudia?' she heard Julian call after her.

She turned at the door and smiled sweetly at him. 'Yes?'

There was a puzzled frown on his face. 'Are you all right?'

'Of course. I'll just be a minute.'

Once she was safely out of sight, she ran lightly down the hall, stopping along the way at the bathroom, where she picked up her toothbrush and comb. In the studio, her handbag was still where she'd dropped it the night before, on the floor near the easel. For one insane moment she contemplated taking up a palette knife and slashing the portrait still sitting there, but restrained herself.

She threw Julian's shirt down on the couch, then, her cheeks burning at the painful reminder, gathered up her discarded underwear and stuffed it in her bag. She moved fast, her one thought to get out of there, out of Julian's house, away from last night's memories and, most of all, away from the sight of Sharon and Julian together.

She sat down on the couch for a second to catch her breath and to consider what to do next. Whatever it was, she wanted to do it with some semblance of dignity. She could call home and ask Peter or Laura to come and get her—or she could even walk across the fields.

She glanced out the window. The rain was coming down steadily in a fine stream, not a downpour, but enough to make her look very foolish if she suddenly announced she'd decided to walk home in it. Although the very idea of calling her family sickened her, that was probably the best way.

There was no telephone in the studio. She'd just have to find one. The living-room, she thought, and rose to her feet. Then she heard the footsteps coming down the hall and went rigid.

Oh, no, she groaned to herself, I can't face him now! But she'd have to. Summoning up every ounce of her dancer's training, she unclenched her tight muscles, ran a hand over her hair, plastered a smile on her face, and started walking towards the door, reaching it just as Julian arrived.

'There you are,' he said. 'Are you sure you're all right?'

'Yes, I'm fine,' she lied through her teeth. 'I was

just going to look for the telephoe.'

'What do you want a telephone for?'

'Oh, I thought I'd see if Laura could come to get me.' She motioned towards the window, where the rain was coming down harder. 'It's not a good day for a walk.'

He knit his brow in a puzzled frown. 'You can't go home,' he stated flatly. 'We're going to spend the day together.'

'Oh?' she asked with the raise of an eyebrow. 'I thought you'd be involved with Sharon the rest of the day. You probably have a lot to do, you know, discussing your exhibition, things like that. I know how important it is to you, how hard you've worked, and she's come all this way, and . . .' Then, to her utter horror, she burst into tears.

'Oh, God!' he breathed, and gathered her into his arms.

She cried noisily and wetly into his chest while he stroked her back and murmured soothing sounds. When the sobs finally showed signs of subsiding, he reached back, pushed the door closed, and led her over to the couch.

He sat down, pulling her along with him, and took out a handkerchief from his back pocket. She turned away from him, ashamed to face him after her childish outburst, but he forced her head around and gently started mopping her face.

'Now,' he said when he was through, 'what's all this about?' He waited, but she couldn't utter a word. 'All right,' he went on in a flat tone, 'let me guess. It's Sharon, isn't it?' When she still didn't answer, Julian sighed and said, 'Let me explain about Sharon. First of all, there is not, nor has there ever been, anything of a physical or romantic nature between us.'

She sniffed loudly. 'No?'

'No. Sharon has been enormously helpful to me in my career. She's a shrewd agent, a fine businesswoman, and she was the first person in the art world who saw value in my work. She arranged my first exhibition, and has seen to it all my paintings commanded the highest possible price.' He spread his hands. 'I owe every success I've ever had to Sharon, and I value our relationship more than I can say. But that's the end of it. It never went further. In the first place, we're both smart enough to know it doesn't work to mix business with pleasure, and in the second place—and even more important—there has never been a spark of attraction between us.'

Claudia didn't believe him for one moment. She had listened attentively to his long speech and, while she could see he meant it when he said there had never been anything between them, it was still obvious to her that Sharon was very definitely attracted to *him*, whether he knew it or not.

But how could he not know it? Was it possible he was able to deliberately blind himself to her seductive behaviour towards him just to maintain the necessary fiction that they were only business partners? Or was he lying to her now?

'I still think I'd better go,' she said at last. 'You really do have business to discuss, that's obvious, or she wouldn't have come all the way up here.'

She stood up and looked down at him. He was sitting on the edge of the couch, his long legs spread apart, his elbows propped on his knees, staring down at the floor. When he looked up at her, there was something in his eyes that caught at her throat. She gazed into the grey depths for a long moment, trying to read what was behind them, and what she saw there frightened her.

It dawned on her then just exactly what she'd done. From the moment Sharon had arrived, she'd immediately jumped to the conclusion that Julian had deceived her, lied to her about Sharon, even flaunted the woman in front of her. But where was the lie?

The one thing he had made perfectly clear to her from the very beginning was that there were to be no strings, no commitment, no future. She had agreed. Now she had broken that agreement with her insane, mindless jealousy. She knew that now. What was more, what she'd just seen in Julian's eyes told her that he knew it, too. Had she lost him?

She didn't know what to do. Should she try to explain? Apologise to him? But why should she? She gazed at him uncertainly, trying to find the words that would make everything all right again.'

But it was too late. He was already on his feet and moving towards the door. 'I'll take you home, then,' he said distantly, 'if you're determined to go.'

She gathered up her bag and followed him out into the hall. On the way, he stopped at the kitchen, where Sharon was still sitting at the table, drinking coffee and leafing through the contents of a manila folder. She looked up when she saw them, her sharp eyes darting from one to the other.

'I'm going to take Claudia home now, Sharon,' Julian said. 'I won't be long.'

The blonde turned to Claudia. 'I hope I'm not running you off,' she said sweetly.

'Not at all,' Claudia replied. 'Business before pleasure.'

They left then, but not before Claudia saw the green eyes harden and the smile disappear.

They spoke very little on the way home. The rain was pelting down by now, and Julian gave all his attention to the road ahead, while Claudia sat in mute misery beside him, listening to the swish of the windscreen wipers and wishing with all her heart she could turn the clock back an hour to the time before Sharon made her appearance.

At the house, she opened her door and turned to him. 'Don't get out. There's no point in both of us getting wet.'

He nodded briefly and said, 'I'll call you.'

She got out of the car and ran through the rain to the shelter of the porch. Even before she reached the top of the steps, he had turned the car around and was racing up the driveway. She looked after him until he disappeared, then opened the door and went inside.

Claudia moped around the house the rest of the morning, straightening the drawers of her dresser, sorting through her autumn clothes and doing hand laundry. After lunch she did her nails, leafed through several magazines, and finally, in desperation, turned on the television set to a game show.

She was slouched on the couch in the living-room, staring dully at the flickering screen, not even hearing the shrieks and laughter of the hyperactive contestants or the endless patter of the unctuous host, when Laura appeared in the doorway, her hands on her hips, her mouth set in a firm line, staring down at her. 'Well?' she said at last, moving into the room.

Claudia looked up at her, ready to ward off the inevitable inquisition, but Laura only sat down beside her and, without another word, reached over and gave her a reassuring pat on the shoulder.

All it took was that one sign of sympathy. Claudia leaned back with a sigh, her eyes squeezed tight against the hot tears that stung behind them. Finally, one trickled down her cheek, and she reached up to brush it away with her hand.

She opened her eyes and said, 'Oh, Laura, I'm such a fool.'

Laura laughed and tucked her legs up underneath her. 'Aren't we all?' she asked lightly. 'Want to talk about it?'

The whole story came pouring out then, her love for Julian, his clearly stated determination not to commit himself, Sharon's appearance at breakfast, her resentment of the blonde woman's possessive attitude, culminating in the jealous rage and the tearful scene with Julian.

'And so I've blown it,' she ended up dully. 'This time I've really blown it good. I'll never hear from him again.'

Laura thought a minute, then asked, 'He said he'd call you?' Claudia nodded. 'Well, then,' Laura went on, 'why not give him the benefit of the doubt?'

'Laura,' she said grimly, 'I made an utter, absolute fool of myself. After assuring him over and over again that I could handle what he had to offer, the minute *she* showed up, with her glamour, her hands all over him, just as though she *owned* him, I turned into a whining adolescent.' She shook her head. 'He won't call.'

'I'm still not sure I agree,' Laura said quietly. 'But, whether he does or not, I think there's a far more important issue at stake here.'

'And what's that?'

'I think you should ask yourself very seriously if

you really want to go on with this affair at all.' She shook her head sadly. 'I don't know, Claudia. I just don't think you can tolerate it. You were hurt this time when, according to Julian, there was no reason for it. What will it be like if—or more to the point *when*— you're confronted with a real rival?'

Claudia sighed harshly. 'Considering the way I behaved this morning, it won't be pretty.' Then her face clouded over again. 'But what can I do? I love him.'

'Only you can decide that, but sometimes, dear, it's wiser to give up what you know you can't have before you're forced into it.' She stood up and reached down a hand. 'Come on, let's go have a nice cup of good strong tea. And I wouldn't grieve too much for Julian. If I'm any judge of men, he'll call you, just as he said he would.'

Laura turned out to be right, but only after Claudia had spent one long, sleepless night and most of the next day in an agony of uncertainty, half certain he wouldn't call, half hoping he would, and jumping every time the telephone rang.

Then, late the next afternoon, when she heard his voice at the other end of the line, she almost fainted with relief. Then, warning herself sternly to be cool, casual and under no circumstances to breathe one syllable about Sharon, she said a cheerful hello and waited for him to speak.

'I wondered if you'd be interested in going with me down to the harbour to pick up my wandering camper,' he said. 'She's due in about an hour. Then we could all go out to dinner at Martha's Kitchen, if you think you can stand another meal there.'

All go out to dinner? Claudia asked herself. Who

was 'all'? Then, aloud, she said, 'Yes, that sounds fine.'

'All right. See you in fifteen minutes or so, then, OK?'

'Yes. OK.'

After they had hung up, she hurried upstairs to change her clothes, still wondering if Julian's 'all' included Sharon. If so, she decided, she would simply have to swallow it and force herself to be pleasant and courteous to the woman if it killed her.

She waited for him out in front. Yesterday's rain squall had passed by, and the late afternoon sun sparkled in the freshened air. It was a little cool, so she'd worn a sweater over her cotton dress. Then she heard his car coming down the drive. As it came into view, she raised a hand over her eyes and, with a pounding heart, scanned the front seat for any sign of a passenger.

She wasn't positive he was alone until he'd pulled up in front of the house. Then, with a glad smile of welcome, she walked down the steps to meet him.

As he leaned across the seat to open the door for her, she searched his face carefully, but could read nothing there of what he was thinking or feeling. Although his brief smile seemed warm enough, he made no move to touch her, and started the car as soon as she got inside.

He didn't speak until he'd turned on to the cliff road that led into the village. Then he glanced at her and said, 'We've got nearly an hour before Margaret's boat gets in. Would you like to stop and have a drink? Afterwards we can walk down to the dock.'

'Yes. That sounds good.'

Then he added, almost as an afterthought, 'I

wanted to come early because I thought you and I should have a talk.'

Her heart skipped a beat and she didn't say anything for a moment. 'What about?' she asked at last.

'About what happened yesterday.'

He just left that hanging and didn't say anything else all the rest of the way into the village, where he parked the car in front of Martha's. They went inside and sat at a table far back in a dim corner of the cocktail lounge. After the waitress took their order, he settled back in a chair, lit a cigarette, and gazed at her through the wisps of smoke between them.

Claudia had laid both hands flat on the tabletop to keep them from shaking, dreading what was coming, and as she stared down at them, to her surprise he reached out and covered one of them with his. She looked up at him, and he began to speak.

'Claudia,' began Julian softly, 'I think you know how attracted I am to you. I care about you, I really do, as much as I could care for any woman. What we've had together this past month, especially that one wonderful night, has meant a lot to me.'

He frowned, as though at a loss for words, then sighed and ground out his cigarette in the ashtray. The waitress appeared just then with their drinks, and Claudia took a grateful swallow of her sherry. So far it hadn't been so bad, but she knew he was leading up to something that very well could be.

'What are you trying to say, Julian?' she asked quietly.

'It's not easy,' he replied with a rueful smile. 'I don't like to be in a position of setting down rules.' Then he gave her a direct look. 'But I thought I'd made my position clear right from the beginning.

What's more, you were quite certain you could handle it. At least, that's what you told me several times.'

'You're talking about what happened the other day,' she said. 'When Sharon showed up.' She leaned forward and said earnestly, 'I should have explained then. Please try to understand. It was so—so embarrassing to have her find me there, sitting in your kitchen that early in the morning, knowing what she must be thinking. I've never been in that position before. I got confused. And then, when I saw you together, I thought . . .' She broke off and looked away.

'I know what you thought, and I did my best to reassure you that it wasn't true. Didn't I?' She nodded miserably, still unable to face him. 'Look at me, Claudia,' he said in a harsh, commanding tone, and she turned to face him, her eyes wide.

'Don't speak to me that way, Julian,' she said slowly. 'I don't like it.'

'I'm sorry,' he said stiffly. 'I apologise. But can't you see, we've got to get this thing straightened out now, before we go any further?'

A slow anger had begun to build in Claudia's heart and mind. He was making her feel like a disobedient child being scolded by the teacher. She raised her glass and took another swallow of her sherry, then set it down carefully on the table. As she did, she noticed that her hands were no longer shaking.

She looked at him. 'Go on,' she said in an even voice.

His eyebrows lifted slightly, but if he was taken aback by her tone he covered it well. 'I can't tolerate that kind of emotional upset,' he went on. 'It's bad for my work, and I've already told you that comes first.'

His work, she seethed inwardly. He's darned lucky he's *got* work to do. What about *my* work? How would he feel if he had to give up his precious painting, as I did my dancing? At that moment, all she wanted to do was get up and get out of there, and she was just about ready to ask him to take her home when he polished off the last of his drink and half rose out of his char.'

'It's time to go get Margaret,' he said.

She knew then that she couldn't go. Someone had to be there when the girl got off the boat. She watched him as he stood up and came over to pull her chair back. As he did, he leaned over to kiss the back of her neck, his lips cold from the drink he'd just finished. She rose quickly.

He put his hands on her shoulders and smiled down at her, the familiar gleam shining out of the depths of his grey eyes. 'Then we understand each other?' he said in a soft, seductive tone.

She returned his smile. 'Oh, yes, Julian,' she said calmly. 'I think we understand each other quite well.'

For Margaret's sake, she did walk down to the boat dock with Julian, and after picking her up they all went back to Martha's. By sheer will-power, Claudia managed to get through the seemingly endless dinner without screaming. Luckily, the meal was entirely taken up anyway with the girl's endless happy chatter about her experiences at camp.

When they were through and went back outside, it was past eight o'clock and growing dark. They got inside the car, all three in the front seat, with Margaret between them, and as soon as Julian started the car Claudia made up her mind.

Making her voice light and casual, she said, 'I'm

sure Margaret's tired and grubby after her busy weekend, and would like to have a bath and get straight to bed. So why don't you just drop me off on the way, Julian?'

Margaret immediately began to protest loudly, but Claudia could tell her heart wasn't in it. Her eyelids were already drooping and she was leaning heavily against her.

'Oh, come on, Margaret!' Julian said with a laugh. 'You're dead on your feet and you know it. You can see all you want of Claudia tomorrow.'

Claudia felt a sharp pang of guilt at that. She hated to disappoint the girl just because her father was such a beast, but if she backed down now she knew she'd be lost. She didn't have to make any promises, after all. She put her arm around the girl and gave her a quick squeeze.

'We'll see,' was all she said.

In less than five minutes they were at her house. She got out of the car and leaned over at the open window. 'Goodnight, then,' she said to Margaret. 'Pleasant dreams.' Then she looked at Julian who was still wearing his fatuous, pleased expression at the tidy way things had turned out. 'Goodbye, Julian,' she said tonelessly, then turned and hurried up to the house.

When she got inside, she went into the living-room to let Peter and Laura know she was home. Peter was settled back in his easy chair, his eyes firmly glued to the baseball game on the television. Laura sat on the couch, knitting. She looked up when she saw Claudia.

'You're home early,' she remarked with a smile. 'Did Julian's little girl get home safely?'

'Yes,' Claudia replied. 'She was awfully tired,

though, so we decided Julian should take her straight home to bed.' She covered her mouth and yawned convincingly. 'I'm rather beat myself. Think I'll go turn in now.'

Laura nodded. 'Goodnight, then.'

Claudia went down the hall and up the stairs. In her bedroom she opened the top drawer of her desk and took out her address book, then went back out on to the landing to the upstairs telephone extension. Slowly, her heart thudding, she dialled the long-distance number, then leaned against the wall for support while it rang.

He didn't answer until the sixth ring. Then there wa a click and a familiar voice said, 'Hello.'

'Hello, Charles,' she said. 'It's Claudia. I'm sorry to call so late.'

'No problem. It's good to hear from you. How are you?'

'I'm fine.' She paused and took a deep breath. 'Charles,' she went on, 'are either or both of your offers still on?'

'Sure are,' he said at once. 'When can you leave?'

'How about tomorrow?'

CHAPTER TEN

CLAUDIA stood at her office window looking out at the steep hills of San Francisco. It was just five o'clock, and down on the street below office workers were pouring out of their buildings and scurrying in all directions to their bus stops. The morning fog had burned off by now, but there were still faint wisps of haze over the bay, and a hint of autumn in the air. She crossed her bare arms over in front of her and rubbed her hands over them.

Hard to believe she'd been back in the city for a whole month. After a week at Charles's sister's house, she'd found her own apartment not far from the theatre where the ballet company had its studios.

She felt quite at home here. In the background behind her she could hear the familiar sounds of the practice rooms, the thumping of a tinny piano in a steady, exaggerated beat, the thud of the students' slippered feet coming down hard on the bare wooden floor, and a woman's voice in the beginners' class.

With a little sigh she turned and walked to her desk. She'd been interviewing late applicants for that year's classes all afternoon, and there were still appointments to come that evening.

Just as she sat down, Charles appeared at the door. 'How about grabbing a bite to eat?' he asked.

Claudia looked up at him and smiled. Dressed as always in a neat three-piece suit, his blond hair slicked down, he lookd every inch the successful business manager.

She frowned down at her cluttered desk. 'Oh, I'd better not. I've got evening appointments starting at seven and I still haven't finished writing up my notes.' She made a face. 'Although I don't know if I can face one more eager mother pushing her Sally or Joanne at me and telling me what remarkable natural talents their daughters possess.'

He laughed. 'Come on. Sounds to me like you need a break. You have to eat, and the fresh air will do you good.'

'Maybe you're right.' She stood up, took her jacket off the back of her chair and slipped it over her shoulders. 'But I have to be back by seven.'

He nodded. 'No problem. That gives us almost two hours. Are you in the mood for Chinese or Italian?'

She thought a minute. 'Both, actually. I'm starved. You decide.'

'OK, then, Chinese it is.'

They walked past the studios that lined the long hallway, to the tunes of *Les Sylphides* and *Swan Lake* fighting it out from either side, then rode down on the creaky elevator in companionable silence.

Out on the street it was a little cooler than it had looked from five storeys up, with a brisk breeze blowing through the Golden Gate. At the entrance to the building, Claudia stopped to put on her jacket, and Charles was immediately behind her, helping her, his hands lingering for a second on her shoulders when he was through.

They started walking along the crowded street up the two blocks to the Ming Tree, dawdling along the way so that Claudia could look in the shop windows, one of her favourite pastimes since she'd been back in the bustling city. The theatre was located in a rather offbeat neighbourhood, with interesting shops and ethnic restaurants.

There was an antique jewellery store, a bookshop that catered to arcane tastes, with a large map of the zodiac prominently displayed in the front window, and a little farther on a Greek café.

At the first corner they had to stop for the pedestrian-crossing lights. When it turned green they started across the intersection, and as they approached the kerb on the other side, Claudia's eye was caught by a familiar bright object in the window of the art gallery on the corner. As they came closer she was certain.

There in the window, all by itself and sitting on an easel, was one of the colourful still-life paintings she'd seen in Julian's studio just over a month ago. Propped up against the easel on the floor was a large engraved card that read: 'Julian Graves Exhibition, September 12—13'.

She turned hot, then cold, then averted her eyes and hurried on past the gallery. 'We'd better get moving,' she said to a bewildered Charles, who was hurrying to catch up with her.

'What's wrong?' he asked, peering down into her face. 'You look as though you've just seen a ghost.'

In a way she had, but she wasn't going to tell Charles that. She only smiled at him and kept on moving. Thank God there had been no sign of Julian at the gallery. The exhibition didn't open for two days, and she'd simply avoid that corner of the street until it was safely over.

The Ming Tree was crowded, as usual, and they were given the last table. As soon as they were seated and Claudia had sliped off her jacket, the harried Chinese waiter came to take their order. They both decided on the combination plate, and, when he asked if they wanted drinks before dinner, Charles gave Claudia an enquiring glance. She thought a moment, then annouced she'd have a Martini.

When the waiter was gone, Charles was still staring at her. 'Since when have you started drinking Martinis?' he asked. 'I thought sherry was more your style.'

'Blame it on the doting mamas and their oh, so talented offspring,' she said with a nervous laugh. 'It just seemed like a good idea for a change. Don't worry, Charles. I'm not becoming addicted.'

He stared pensively at her for a moment, then leaned acrosss the table to put his head close to hers. 'No,' he said in a low voice, 'but you do get lovelier every time I see you.' When she frowned slightly, he settled back in his chair and held up both hands. 'Don't panic,' he said jokingly. 'I'm not going to push.'

'Oh, Charles,' she said with a sigh. 'You make me feel like such a heartless, ungrateful beast.'

'Well, you are!' he said, only half kidding. He shook his head. 'You already know how I feel anyway, so why should it bother you if I say it? Besides, I like to say it.'

'But I'm not sure I like hearing it,' she said, with a wry twist to her mouth.

He shook his head. 'I just wish I knew what it would take, Claudia, to convince you to give in and marry me.'

Only a pair of haunted grey eyes with black flecks in them, she thought bitterly. Only a tall dark man who won't allow himself to feel and who doesn't want me.

'Charles, I'm sorry,' she said aloud. 'But what can

I do? I'm very fond of you, you know that quite well, but you're too fine a man to have to settle for second best. I don't know. Sometimes I think the accident last fall crippled more than my leg. At least, nothing has come along to replace dancing in my life.'

That wasn't quite true, she thought guiltily, and added to herself, at least, nothing she could have. One man had broken through her defenses. But never again!

'I'll settle for anything I can get,' Charles said with firm conviction. 'And I wish you'd give up calling yourself crippled, in any way, shape or form. I was just noticing this evening as we walked along that your limp is so much improved it isn't even noticeable any more.'

She brightened at that. 'Yes. I'm so pleased with my progress. Although I couldn't have done it alone. Without you and my family and Jenny, I'd still be hiding away up on the island, sulking in my room and feeling sorry for myself.'

'I doubt that very much.'

'Maybe so, but it would have taken much longer without the support of people who cared about me, and I do appreciate the part you played in that, Charles. You must believe that. And I wish it could be more,' she added softly. 'I really do.'

'Well, not to worry. I'm a patient type, and perhaps in time it *will* be more.'

They finished dinner early and Claudia was back in her office by six-thirty, stuffed with chow mein and sweet and sour pork, and in plenty of time to finish up her notes on the day's applicants while she waited for her first appointment of the evening at seven o'clock.

On the way back to the studio from the restaurant, she'd kept her eyes firmly averted as they passed by the art gallery on the corner. Now that the first shock of seeing Julian's painting in the window was over, she decided there was no reason why she should hide from him, anyway. He was nothing to her any more, and she was certainly nothing to him.

She still couldn't quite banish the memory of that last awful conversation, though, or of the fatuous, self-satisfied smirk on his face when she'd left him that night. He'd been so sure of himself, so convinced of her slavish love, her craving to please him, that he was utterly convinced his hurtful lecture to her about no strings had settled the matter once and for all.

She stared into space, her pencil tapping on the desk. He'd been so smug, she thought bitterly, and she wished for the hundredth time she could have been there to see his face when he'd received her letter, or even when he'd called and Laura told him she'd left Hidden Harbour and gone to San Francisco and wouldn't be back.

She'd never forget that night after he and Margaret had left her in front of the house and she'd called Charles, how she'd dashed back to her bedroom, thrown her clothes in a suitcase, then gone back downstairs to announce her plans to a bewildered Peter and a silent sympathising Laura.

She'd written the letter late that night, when Peter and Laura had gone to bed and the house was silent. It was short and to the point, and she could still remember it word for word! 'Julian, by the time you get this I'll be back in San Francisco. Please don't try to contact me. It's much better this way. Things would hever have worked out between us. Try to explain to Margaret and give her my love. Claudia.'

She'd dropped it off at the post office when Peter drove her to the ferry terminal early the next morning. That was a month ago. She hadn't expected to hear from him—not with his overabundance of male pride—and so she hadn't. The past month had been difficult. A man like Julian Graves was not easy to forget, but Laura had been right when she'd said it was better in the long run to give up what you couldn't have, before you were forced into it, anyway. Claudia enjoyed her work, and she had found a certain peace.

There was a knock on her door just then, and a short, plump young girl came into the room. It was Kitty, the night receptionist, and she had another file folded in her hand. 'Your seven o'clock appointment is here, Claudia.'

'Thanks, Kitty. Which one is it?'

Kitty glanced at the folder. 'Martindale. Girl, twelve years old. Mother in tow.' She looked at Claudia and grinned.

Claudia rolled her eyes in exasperation. 'Why can't the admissions people do a better job of weeding out?' she asked. 'They know quite well twelve is too old for a beginner.'

Kitty shrugged, dropped the file on Claudia's desk, and made for the door. 'Ours not to reason why,' she called over her shoulder. 'I'll send them in.'

As it turned out, the Martindale girl had had five years of lessons, and when Claudia put her through the basic positions she looked quite promising. At the end of the session, she rose to her feet and extended a hand to the anxious mother.

'I'm going to recommend acceptance, Mrs Martindale,' she said.

When the grateful pair had thanked her effusively and left, Claudia made a notation in the file, 'Accepted,' and set it on top of the others. Then she buzzed for Kitty to send in the next applicant, and for the next two hours she sat and watched one unacceptable after another.

When the last one was gone, she sighed and stretched with weariness. It was after nine o'clock, and it had been a long day. With one last rueful glance at her cluttered desk, she shoved her chair back, and looked up to see Kitty standing at the door again.

'How did it go?' she asked.

'Not bad,' Claudia replied. 'One acceptable out of four is a fair percentage. That Martindale girl was quite good.' She rose to her feet and reached for her jacket.

'Er—sorry, Claudia,' Kitty mumbled. 'There's one more.'

'Oh, no. I thought you said there were only four. Can't it wait tomorrow? I'm dead beat.'

Kitty shrugged and opened her mouth, but Claudia made a face and broke in before she could get a word out. 'I know. Don't say it. "Ours not to reason why." ' She sat back down. 'Send them in.'

Kitty grinned and set the file folder down on the desk. After she had left, Claudia glanced down at the folder and, when she saw the name 'Graves' written on the front in Kitty's flowing script, she felt all the blood draining out of her face, and her whole body began to tremble from head to toe.

Before she could really absorb the significance of it, she heard footsteps and looked up to see Margaret coming into the room, her sober, stern-faced father behind her. Claudia couldn't move. She just sat there, staring, her heart pounding so hard she was certain he could hear it, until finally Margaret walked over to the desk and stood looking at her, an anxious, dead-serious expression on her small face.

'Claudia, Daddy says I'm not to expect any favours just because we're friends,' she said solemnly.

Claudia glanced up at Julian. He nodded briefly. 'Hello, Claudia,' was all he said.

'Hello, Julian,' she replied, relieved to hear how steady and even her voice sounded. Maybe it wasn't going to be so bad, after all. She turned to Margaret with a smile. 'Your father is right, Margaret,' she said gently. 'It wouldn't be fair to you or the studio to play favourites. If I recommend your acceptance, I promise you it will only be because I think you're good enough. Now, let's see what you can do.'

Julian smiled down at his daughter. 'Good luck, honey,' he said in an encouraging tone. 'I'll be right outside, waiting for you.' He nodded briefly at Claudia again, then turned and walked out of the room.

By the end of the session, Claudia knew the girl was by far one of the best candidates she'd interviewed in the past two weeks. The natural grace and absolutely perfect bone structure she'd noticed during the summer had been well channelled by her dancing classes at the village community centre. She still had a long way to go, of course, but she was at a perfect age to start.

The trouble was, Claudia didn't want her father anywhere near the studio, and if she accepted the girl there would always be that danger. Seeing Julian tonight had brought back all the old pain, all the longings she thought she'd conquered at last, and only his total absence from her life could ever heal that wound permanently.

She looked at the girl, who was gazing up at her expectantly. Claudia knew quite well how she was feeling at that moment. She'd gone through the same thing years ago when she was about the same age, yearning for acceptance, for some sign that what she wanted to do most in the world was really possible, needing encouragement. She knew then that, no matter what her personal feelings were, she couldn't hurt Margaret.

She smiled and put a hand on top of the girl's head. 'OK, Margaret. You're in,' she said, and the relief in the girl's eyes, so much like her father's, was enough to convince Claudia she'd done the right thing. 'You can leave now,' she went on. 'Your father will want to hear the good news.'

As she watched the girl skip happily out of the room, it dawned on Claudia for the first time that Julian would indeed be pleased at his daughter's success, and she wondered what had changed his cold, remote attitude towards the girl. Thinking back, she realised that the change had really started well before she'd left, but had been so gradual she hadn't really taken it in.

Perhaps he's human after all, she thought. She was pleased for Margaret's sake, but it didn't mean anything to her.

She waited in her office another half-hour, making her notes on the evening's appointments, but primarily so she wouldn't have to see Julian again. It was after ten o'clock before she laid her pencil down. Everyone else had gone home. When she put on her jacket, switched off the light and went down the silent empty hallway to the elevator, there was no sign of him.

* * *

ONE STOLEN MOMENT 181

As the days passed, the memory of that night gradually faded, and once again Claudia began to feel safe. Although she saw Margaret occasionally at the studio, they rarely spoke. Claudia felt it would be bad for the girl if she showed her any favouritism at all, and apparently Julian had instructed her along the same lines.'

Then one night, about two weeks later, he simply appeared. She had worked late again, and it was after ten by the time she got home to her apartment house on Telegraph Hill. She was walking down the long, dimly lit hallway to her own apartment, and had stopped for a moment to reach into her handbag and fish out her keys. When she looked up again, there he was, leaning up against her door, waiting for her.

She stopped short. Her first impulse was to turn and run. Then she thought, no, damn it. Why should I? It's *my* apartment! She raised her chin, squared her shoulders and continued on, his eyes burning into her every long step of the way.

'Hello, Julian,' she said coolly when she reached him. She bent over to put her key in the lock. 'What brings you here?'

'I want to talk to you,' he said in a low voice.

She looked at him. 'Sorry, Julian, but we have nothing to talk about, and what *you* want no longer interests me.'

He pushed himself away from the door and straightened up, his tall form looming over her. 'You left Hidden Harbour without a word,' he said in an accusing tone.

'Didn't you get my letter?'

He dismissed the letter with an impatient wave of his hand. 'I don't call that cold note an explanation,' he said. 'You might have written that to a total stranger. And I think you owe me that explanation.'

The hot anger rose up in her and she glared at him. 'I owe you nothing,' she bit out. 'Nothing at all. Now go away. I'm tired. I've had a long day.'

She turned the key in the lock, pushed the door open and went inside, but before she could get it closed he had slipped through behind her, shut the door, and now stood leaning back against it.

Claudia flipped on the light switch and turned to face him. 'Get out, Julian,' she said. 'Please. Just go away.'

'I'm not going until we've had this thing out once and for all,' he said flatly.

'There's nothing *to* have out. Can't you understand?'

'I'm not leaving until you tell me why you disappeared that way,' he went on, just as if she hadn't spoken. 'I have the right to know.'

She was almost trembling with fury now, and her voice quavered ominously when she could finally speak. 'You have no rights whatsoever, as far as I'm concerned.'

Then, to her utter astonishment, his face fell. As the proud, arrogant expression slowly faded, he ran a hand over his black hair and gazed down at her with a look that would have been pleading in a humbler man.

'I know I'm thick about such things,' he said at last. 'But even I have a pretty good idea why you did it.' He forced her to meet his eyes. 'I was pretty high-handed in setting down my rules for our relationship, wasn't I? And pretty stupid, too.'

He was getting to her again. She knew it. She could feel it, the mesmerising pull of those haunted grey eyes, the fine features, the sheer, utterly overwhelming *maleness* of the man.

'Julian,' she said wearily. 'Don't. Please don't.'

As though he could sense her weakening, he pressed on. 'Give me twenty minutes. That's all I ask. Then, if you still want me to go, I will, and I promise I'll never bother you again.'

She bit her lip and looked down at her feet. It would be insanity to let him stay for *two* minutes, let alone twenty. She'd deserve everything she got if she agreed. She couldn't go through that again. She looked at him, all prepared to refuse.

'Twenty minutes,' he said quietly, the grey eyes boring into her.

'Oh, all right,' she said. 'But that's all.' He nodded. 'And then you promise you'll go?' He nodded again. 'Come on, then, we'd better sit down.'

He followed her meekly into the small living-room. She pointed at a chair by the window, then went over to the couch across from it. He remained standing, his hands in the pockets of his trousers, staring intently into space. Then he turned to her.

'You don't have anything to drink, do you?' he asked hopefully. 'A beer? A glass of wine?'

She glared at him in exasperation. Wouldn't you know it? she thought wryly. Just like a man to press his advantage once he'd gained one small concession!

'No,' she said firmly. 'I don't. She sat down on the couch and glanced at her watch. 'You've already used up three minutes.'

He crossed over to the couch in two long strides and, before she could protest, he'd planted himself firmly down right next to her. He sat there for a few moments, his elbows on his thighs, his hands clasped loosely between his knees, gazing down at the floor, apparently gathering his thoughts.

Claudia glanced over at him. He was sitting far too close, their bodies almost touching, but instead of moving away, as she knew she should, she soon found herself staring at the faint, dark stubble on his lean cheeks, the little pulse that throbbed along his bony jaw; and, when he suddenly turned, she jumped a little.

'I'm not quite sure where to begin,' he said.

Annoyed at having been caught staring at him, she retorted tartly, 'Why not try the morning Sharon showed up?' The minute the words were out of her mouth she knew she'd made a serious tactical error by the gleam of satisfaction in his eye and the slow smile that curved on his lips.

'Ah, Sharon,' he said. 'I explained to you about Sharon once. But I see you didn't believe me.'

'It doesn't matter,' she said softly.

He wrinkled his brow. 'But it does. Did you think I was lying when I told you there'd never been anything between us?'

'I guess not,' she replied grudgingly.

'Well, that's a start.' He paused for a moment, then went on slowly, 'I've had a lot of time to think in the past month, Claudia, and the unhappy conclusion I finally came to was that I treated you very badly right from the beginning, from the way I reacted to the news about your accident, to the silly stand I took about your perfectly natural jealousy of Sharon.'

'I was *not* jealous of Sharon!' she exclaimed hotly.

He gave her a bewildered look. 'No? Well, what upset you so that morning at my house when she showed up?'

'I just . . .' She swallowed, searching for words, then cleared her throat. 'I just didn't like the way she—the way you——' She turned on him then. 'All right,' she said with a sigh, 'I was jealous. I'm sorry. I was wrong.'

He reached over and took her hand in his, holding it on his thigh, which felt very hard and strong underneath it. 'No, you weren't wrong. You had every right to be upset. I've dealt with Sharon for so long, and been so dependent on her in a business way, that it just never occurred to me how it might look to you.'

He had turned her hand over, palm up, and was stroking it softly. She knew she should take it away, but something held her motionless. A strange, tinglig sensation rippled along her skin, and her heartbeat was beginning to pick up dangerously.

'After Sharon left that afternoon—which, by the way, was the same day she got there—I thought over what had happened, why you were so upset, and then it occurred to me that you might be falling in love with me.' He put her hand up to his mouth and pressed it against his lips. 'God forgive me, I panicked.' He turned to her. 'I'd told you about my marriage, how I felt about my wife before she died, the accident that killed her, and my vow never, ever, under any circumstances, to become emotionally entangled with a woman again.'

She nodded. 'Yes,' she said dully. She wished he would finish what he had to say and get out. They'd gone all over this ground before, and she didn't want to hear it again, especially not when his hand was doing such wonderful things to hers.

'Then,' he went on, 'the next day, when we went to pick up Margaret at the boat, I felt I had to set the record straight again, just so there would be no possible misunderstanding between us. My behaviour was boorish and probably unforgivable, but at the time, of course, I didn't see it that way. I thought I was being very rational, very sensible. But after you left the island the way you did—well, everything changed.'

She still wasn't sure what he was leading up to, so she remained silent, waiting to hear what he would say next.

Finally, he sighed. 'What I'm trying in my feeble way to do, Claudia, is to ask you to forgive me.'

She suddenly realised that he had moved closer to her during his long recitation, and his leg burned all along the length of it where it touched his. 'Yes, of course,' she muttered. 'I forgive you.' She pulled her hand away and rose abruptly to her feet. 'Now, your twenty minutes is up. I did what you asked. I listened to you. You said you'd leave.'

As she looked down at him, their eyes met. 'Look,' he said, 'I don't blame you for despising me, but please, Claudia, please don't send me away. Give me a chance to make it up to you.'

'What do you mean?'

Without a word, he reached up, took her by the arm and pulled her back down beside him. The next thing she knew, his arms were around her and his mouth pressing on hers in a long, passionate kiss. For a moment she struggled to be free, but after a few moments her lips parted, and she went limp against him.

He tore his mouth away, put his cheek against hers and breathed into her ear, 'God, I've missed you, Claudia.' He raised his head, put his hands on her shoulders and gazed down into her eyes. 'I'll never forget that one night we had together,' he said softly. 'The night I held you naked in my arms. I've wanted you, ached for you, every night since. And I know you want me, too.'

She twisted her head and pulled away, hardly trusting herself to speak. She was so tempted. She could have him back. Finally, she turned to face him. 'Of course I still want you. You know that quite well, but you shouldn't take advantage of that. Nothing has really changed.'

'Yes, it had. *I've* changed. It finally sank into my thick head that, by protecting myself against involvement, I risked losing the one thing I really wanted. *Had* lost it, in fact, unless I could talk my way back into your life.'

'Julian,' she whispered, 'what are you trying to say?'

'Hell, Claudia, I'm trying to tell you I was wrong to set down a line we couldn't cross. I'm trying to tell you I can't live without you. In fact, what I'm really trying to say is that I love you.' He smiled. 'There, now, it's out. I love you.'

Claudia could hardly believe her ears. Julian loves me, she thought happily. But what did that mean? She had to find out. He could have more rules up his sleeve.

'I don't know, Julian,' she said slowly. 'I'm not sure I want to risk that kind of hurt ever again.'

'Well, then, there's Margaret,' he said solemnly.

'Margaret? What does Margeret have to do with it?'

He shrugged. 'The poor child needs a mother.'

Poor child, indeed! Since when was he so concerned . . . Then the words sank in. She looked at him. He was smiling at her, an amused, pleased smile of complacency.

'Marry me, darling,' he said. 'I love you and I need you desperately. But if that doesn't sway you, do it for Margaret.'

'Oh, you fool!' she cried, and fell into his arms.

His hands were busy at the buttons of her blouse. 'Tell me you want me as much as I want you,' he breathed.

'Yes, yes. Of course I do.' She had trouble getting the words out, because his hands were working their magic on her bare breasts by now, his fingers trailing in hot little circles around the aroused peaks. Eagerly and without shame, she undid his shirt and placed her lips on his muscled shoulder, his broad chest, until with a low groan he raised her up and covered her face with kisses.

'Do you love me a little?' he asked a few moments later.

'Oh, a little.'

His mouth moved downwards and he nipped gently at the soft, white skin. 'How about a lot?' he murmured against her breast.

'OK,' she agreed. 'A lot.'

'And you'll marry me?'

'Of course. I couldn't leave Margaret motherless, could I?'

He laughed and crushed her to him, and, as their lips met again, Claudia thought happily that there was no more need for stolen moments, not with this man, not ever again.

Enjoy one beautiful romance after another this holiday.

A holiday provides the perfect opportunity to immerse yourself in a heady new affair and with the Mills and Boon Holiday Romance Pack you'll be spoilt for choice.

In this special selection you'll find four brand new novels from popular writers Emma Darcy, Sandra Field, Jessica Steele and Violet Winspear.

The collection is unique as well as being excellent value for money and will slip easily into your suitcase.

We think you'll find the combination irresistibly attractive.

Just like so many of our leading male characters.

Published July 1988.   **Mills & Boon**   Price £4.80.

Available from Boots, Martins, John Menzies, W H Smith, Woolworths and other paperback stockists.

SPOT THE COUPLE
AND WIN A
£1,000
REAL PEARL NECKLACE

PLUS 10 PAIRS OF REAL PEARL EAR STUDS WORTH OVER £100 EACH

A

B

No piece of jewellery is more romantic than the soft glow and lustre of a real pearl necklace, pearls that grow mysteriously from a grain of sand to a jewel that has a romantic history that can be traced back to Cleopatra and beyond.

To enter just study Photograph A showing a young couple. Then look carefully at Photograph B showing the same section of the river. Decide where you think the couple are standing and mark their position with a cross in pen.

Complete the entry form below and mail your entry PLUS TWO OTHER "SPOT THE COUPLE" Competition Pages from June, July or August Mills and Boon paperbacks, to Spot the Couple, Mills and Boon Limited, Eton House, 18/24 Paradise Road, Richmond, Surrey, TW9 1SR, England. All entries must be received by December 31st 1988.

RULES
1. This competition is open to all Mills & Boon readers with the exception of those living in countries where such a promotion is illegal and employees of Mills & Boon Limited, their agents, anyone else directly connected with the competition and their families.
2. This competition applies only to books purchased outside the U.K. and Eire.
3. All entries must be received by December 31st 1988.
4. The first prize will be awarded to the competitor who most nearly identifies the position of the couple as determined by a panel of judges. Runner-up prizes will be awarded to the next ten most accurate entries.
5. Competitors may enter as often as they wish as long as each entry is accompanied by two additional proofs of purchase. Only one prize per household is permitted.
6. Winners will be notified during February 1989 and a list of winners may be obtained by sending a stamped addressed envelope marked "Winners" to the competition address.
7. Responsibility cannot be accepted for entries lost, damaged or delayed in transit. Illegible or altered entries will be disqualified.

ENTRY FORM

Name _____

Address _____

_____

I bought this book in TOWN _____ COUNTRY _____

This offer applies only to books purchased outside the UK & Eire.
You may be mailed with other offers as a result of this application.